WITCH WOMAN

The Ambrus house was ablaze when I got there, and I could only sit and stare in horror. Then suddenly George Ambrus was standing in front of my carriage, pointing an accusing finger at me. "The witch. The young witch, Mrs. Dunbar's niece. She started the fire. She burned by mother to death. She did it." He picked up a stone and threw it at me.

Now everyone's attention switched from the fire to me. "So she's the one," a male voice commented. "We don't want anymore o' them here." His statement was followed by another stone, and then the crowd was surging toward me and an avalanche of stones began to strike. . . .

More Gothic Novels from SIGNET

- [ ] **BRIDAL BLACK** by Dorothy Daniels. (#E9211—$1.75)
- [ ] **THE CORMAC LEGEND** by Dorothy Daniels. (#J8655—$1.95)*
- [ ] **THE CLIFFS OF DREAD** by Virginia Coffman. (#E8301—$1.75)*
- [ ] **THE HIGH TERRACE** by Virginia Coffman. (#W8228—$1.50)
- [ ] **ISLE OF THE UNDEAD** by Virginia Coffman. (#W8032—$1.50)
- [ ] **MIST AT DARKNESS** by Virginia Coffman. (#Q6138—95¢)
- [ ] **SIGNET DOUBLE GOTHIC—CURSE OF THE ISLAND POOL** by Virginia Coffman and **THE HIGH TERRACE** by Virginia Coffman. (#J9126—$1.95)*
- [ ] **SIGNET DOUBLE GOTHIC—OF LOVE AND INTRIGUE** by Virginia Coffman and **THE CHINESE DOOR** by Virginia Coffman. (#J9313—$1.95)*
- [ ] **THE LANDSEND TERROR** by Julia Trevelyan. (#E8526—$1.75)*
- [ ] **GREYTHORNE** by Julia Trevelyan. (#W7802—$1.50)
- [ ] **THE TOWER ROOM** by Julia Trevelyan. (#E8711—$1.75)*
- [ ] **SIGNET DOUBLE GOTHIC—CHATEAU OF SHADOWS** by Monica Heath and **THE LEGEND OF CROWN POINT** by Monica Heath. (#J7754—$1.95)
- [ ] **CLANCUMARA'S KEEP** by Monica Heath. (#E8359—$1.75)*
- [ ] **DUNCRAIG** by Monica Heath. (#W7935—$1.50)
- [ ] **FALCONLOUGH** by Monica Heath. (#W7627—$1.50)

*Price slightly higher in Canada

Buy them at your local bookstore or use this convenient coupon for ordering.

THE NEW AMERICAN LIBRARY, INC.,
P.O. Box 999, Bergenfield, New Jersey 07621

Please send me the SIGNET BOOKS I have checked above. I am enclosing $_____ (please add 50¢ to this order to cover postage and handling). Send check or money order—no cash or C.O.D.'s. Prices and numbers are subject to change without notice.

Name _____

Address _____

City_____ State_____ Zip Code_____

Allow 4-6 weeks for delivery.
This offer is subject to withdrawal without notice.

HOUSE OF SILENCE

by
Dorothy Daniels

A SIGNET BOOK
NEW AMERICAN LIBRARY
TIMES MIRROR

PUBLISHER'S NOTE

This novel is a work of fiction. Names, characters, places, and incidents are either the product of the author's imagination or are used fictitiously, and any resemblance to actual persons, living or dead, events or locales is entirely coincidental.

NAL BOOKS ARE AVAILABLE AT QUANTITY DISCOUNTS WHEN USED TO PROMOTE PRODUCTS OR SERVICES. FOR INFORMATION PLEASE WRITE TO PREMIUM MARKETING DIVISION, THE NEW AMERICAN LIBRARY, INC., 1633 BROADWAY, NEW YORK, NEW YORK 10019.

Copyright © 1980 by Dorothy Daniels

All rights reserved

SIGNET TRADEMARK REG. U.S. PAT. OFF. AND FOREIGN COUNTRIES
REGISTERED TRADEMARK—MARCA REGISTRADA
HECHO EN CHICAGO, U.S.A.

SIGNET, SIGNET CLASSICS, MENTOR, PLUME, MERIDIAN AND NAL Books are published by The New American Library, Inc., 1633 Broadway, New York, New York 10019

First Printing, September, 1980

1 2 3 4 5 6 7 8 9

PRINTED IN THE UNITED STATES OF AMERICA

ONE

Despite my fatigue, I moved briskly along the deeply carpeted corridor of an exclusive hotel just off Fifth Avenue to the door numbered 804—my aunt's suite. An aunt whose existence I'd not been aware of until an hour ago, when I had come home and found a note from her. Its contents were brief, stating merely that she was Mama's sister and asking that I pay her a visit as soon as possible. I would have ignored the note, believing it the work of an irrational individual except that she had enclosed an old daguerreotype taken of my parents when they were young. A duplicate of it sat on the table in our parlor.

I had stayed beside Mama's bed at Bellevue Hospital the last two days. I was not nearly so aware of my exhaustion as I was of the fact that I needed a bath and change of attire. The temperature had been in the upper nineties for a week, which was not unusual for New York City in July. But the accompanying high humidity made it very debilitating. Nonetheless, I left at once for my aunt's hotel after reading the note.

A uniformed maid, young and attractive, answered my knock. After I identified myself, she addressed me in a voice with a lilting French accent. "Please come in, Miss Parris. I will tell your aunt you have arrived."

I followed her through the mirrored foyer, which was decorated with dainty French furniture, and entered a large parlor. The maid asked me to be seated, went to a closed door, and rapped lightly. A feminine voice, low and cultured, bade her enter. She did so, closing the door behind her.

While waiting, I mentally reviewed the contents of the note. It had expressed shock at Mama's accident, and hope that she would soon recover. The accident had occurred two days before. Mama and I had been on our way to board the horse-drawn carriage that would take us back to the Bronx. Suddenly, seemingly without reason, she had left my side in the middle of the block and stepped off the curb, directly into the path of two huge Percherons pulling a loaded beer van.

My screams mingled with those of the others who had seen the accident. The driver was as shaken as the witnesses. There was no way he could have avoided Mama's being trampled by those huge animals. The clerk in a nearby store had the presence of mind to call the hospital. A morbidly curious crowd had gathered. I held Mama's crumpled, unconscious, and bloodied form in my arms.

I had remained at Bellevue Hospital until this afternoon in the hope that Mama would regain consciousness, even though the doctors stated there was only a remote possibility of such a thing happening.

There was no time to dwell on it further, for the bedroom door opened and a mature woman entered the room. Her flowered chiffon tea gown was very full cut and had billowing sleeves that almost reached to the hem, where pink satin-bowed slippers were visible.

Her round, fair face was unlined, and her blond hair, which showed no visible gray, was styled high on her head. Her eyes were blue and alert, like Mama's. Her expression was compassionate as she walked toward me with outstretched arms.

"My dear Nila, thank you for coming. I sent the note immediately after I read of the accident in the newspaper."

Her hands rested on my shoulders as she studied my face. I knew I didn't look my best, but that didn't concern me. My mind was too consumed with thoughts of Mama.

"You are Mrs. Evelyn Dunbar, Mama's sister," I said.

"I am. I was shocked to read about her horrible accident. I don't know how Loretta survived."

"Mama is still unconscious. The doctors hold little hope. I'm praying for a miracle."

"So shall I," she said. She sighed, then added, "I suppose Loretta has never forgiven me."

"Mama never mentioned your name," I said. "Until I read your note, I wasn't aware I had an aunt."

She nodded, as though the news came as no surprise. "I objected to her marriage. Though our family didn't have money, we had social position. I made a good match. My husband had both. And most important, we were madly in love."

"So were Mama and Papa," I said, rising to their defense.

"I know, my dear." Her tone was so contrite I was ashamed I'd taken offense. "I knew Louis. In fact, it was I who introduced him to your mother. He was a charming Frenchman, a magnificent dancer, and he fell in love with Loretta the moment he set eyes on her."

"And Mama with him," I said. "I scarcely remember him, but Mama spoke of him frequently."

"He taught French at Miss Bingham's, not a very lucrative profession. And though he was a dashing figure and a handsome man, he was not strong."

"I don't recall Mama saying that. I know he drowned."

"Yes," my aunt reminisced. "Not too far from shore, either."

"Did you see my parents after their marriage?"

"No. As I already stated, I objected to the marriage. I was the elder by five years, and we were raised by a spinster aunt. She, as well as I, didn't wish your mama to marry a poor man. However, once they married, we were willing to let bygones be bygones. But your mama never forgave us. I missed her terribly, for we were very close as youngsters."

"Why did you ask me to come here?" Now that I knew the story, I sided with Mama.

"To intercede for me. Ask your mama to forgive me and let me visit her. I have carried a burden of guilt for too many years. I deserved it, but I am truly penitent."

"She isn't even conscious, Mrs. Dunbar," I replied.

"Please don't call me Mrs. Dunbar," she said. "I am your aunt. And—more than anything—I want forgiveness."

"If you live here, why didn't you try to see Mama before?"

"I tried for two years after her marriage to Louis. I tried again when he died. You were just four years old. He died on your birthday."

"So Mama told me," I said. "It happened during a picnic at a lake. Papa went in for a swim, and though an excellent swimmer, he drowned."

My aunt nodded. "I begged Loretta to come live with me. I was already widowed and lonely. To correct a misimpression on your part, I do not live here. I come to New York twice a year to shop."

"Then it was a coincidence that you happened to be in the city."

"Not entirely. I knew you were to graduate from Miss Bingham's Academy last week, and I came to attend the ceremony."

"Miss Bingham allowed me to attend classes as if I were enrolled in the school."

"Which you were," my aunt replied kindly. "I saw to that, though your mother never knew. She'd not have permitted it."

"Are you the reason we had such pleasant living quarters?" I asked.

"Please don't tell Loretta. I loved her. I couldn't

House of Silence

bear to think of her doing menial tasks. Each year I gave a generous endowment to the school, plus the cost of your tuition, with the provision it be kept secret. In return you were to be educated, you and your mama were to be given an apartment of your own, and your mama was to be given work which would keep her busy." My aunt smiled reminiscently. "She was a delicate little thing, like a lovely piece of Dresden china."

"She still is," I said. "I can't bear to think of life without her."

"I pray you won't have to," my aunt said.

An idea occurred to me. "Would you like to come to the hospital with me?"

"Yes, indeed. But should Loretta regain consciousness, my presence might do more harm than good."

I could see the logic in that. "I'll go back to the hospital now. There had been no change in her condition when I left. Mama suffered a concussion when her head struck the curb. Then one of those huge horses trod on her, causing severe internal injuries and several broken bones."

"Why did she want to cross the street? The newspaper article said she stepped right into the path of the van."

"I'm as puzzled as you," I said. "There was nothing on the other side of the street to interest us."

I suddenly felt uncomfortable under my aunt's scrutiny.

"Forgive me for staring at you," she said, "but you have deep circles under your eyes. I doubt you have slept since the accident."

"I haven't. I remained at the hospital until this afternoon, when I returned to the academy and found your note. I came here at once."

"A very fatigued, heartsick, and frightened young lady," she said.

"Yes," I agreed.

"Have you eaten?" she asked.

"They brought food to me at the hospital, but I had no appetite for it."

"Then we shall have a light meal here." When I started to protest, she raised a restraining hand. "I insist. You need your strength. When you've eaten, you may go."

The food made me so drowsy I couldn't keep my eyes open. My aunt insisted I go into her bedroom and lie down. I didn't refuse, because I knew I'd probably fall asleep at Mama's bedside if I didn't get some rest.

When I awoke, a dim light was burning in the room. I was startled to see the hands of the clock pointing to midnight. I got up, went into the bathroom, and splashed my face with cold water. I used my aunt's brush to tidy the loose ends of my dark hair. When I entered the parlor, my aunt was sitting before the window in the semidarkness. She got up and came to me.

I eyed her resentfully. "Why did you let me sleep so long?"

"Don't be angry, Nila. You looked ill when you came here. Even that little rest has worked miracles"

"I'm going back to the hospital," I said.

"There is a carriage waiting for you downstairs. It would please me if you would stay here while Loretta is in the hospital. That way, I could guarantee that you ate and got some rest."

"I'll think about it," I said. "Just now, all I want to do is see Mama."

"I'll pray for her." My aunt picked up my purse and gloves and handed them to me.

I started for the door, but paused long enough to turn back and say, "Thank you, Auntie."

"Thank *you*, Nila." My aunt came to me, embraced me briefly, then sent me on my way.

Ordinarily I'd have been overwhelmed by the luxurious carriage, but now I paid it little heed. I asked the driver to take me to Bellevue as quickly as possible. He told me that Mrs. Dunbar had said the carriage was to be completely at my disposal for as long as I needed it.

I thanked him and sat back. He urged the horse to a fast pace. When he pulled up in front of the hospital, I was out of the carriage before he could alight and assist me.

I ran the length of the main floor and up the stairs to Mama's room. I had almost reached it when a young intern came out.

"Miss Parris," he said softly, "I'm glad you returned. I didn't believe it possible, but your mother is conscious."

"When did it happen?" I asked, angry that I'd not been here.

"Try to relax," he urged gently. "I went in just minutes ago to check her. As I was examining her, she opened her eyes and spoke your name."

"Then there is hope," I exclaimed.

"There is always hope," he said kindly.

I thanked him and walked into Mama's room. The light was dim as I went over to the bed and looked down at Mama. Her head and most of her face were bandaged. I bent and kissed her lightly on the cheek.

Her eyes opened, and she spoke my name again.

"Yes, Mama, I'm here. I'm sorry I left you."

"What . . . day . . . is it?" Her voice was barely audible.

"Friday."

"Tomorrow is your birthday." She spoke haltingly.

I smiled down at her. "My nineteenth. I will bring a cake—we'll celebrate." I kept my voice cheerful, hoping the fear I still had of losing her wasn't evident.

"Where am I, and how did I get here?"

"You're in the hospital. Two horses hauling a van hit you."

"I remember now. Why did I do such a thing?"

I wished I could answer her, but no words came. I

remembered Evelyn Dunbar and decided to risk mentioning her to Mama.

"Your sister sent a note, hoping for quick recovery. She would like to beg forgiveness."

Mama's eyes closed. "I have no sister," she whispered.

"She knew your name and Papa's. Hers is Evelyn Dunbar. She said she had introduced you to Papa, and that he was handsome and a wonderful dancer. She was sorry she objected to your marrying him."

"Louis." Mama's eyes opened. "Louis . . . he was strong. A good swimmer. He should not have drowned."

"No, Mama. It was a dreadful accident."

"No. It was like mine. The horses. I wouldn't have done anything so stupid. Louis wouldn't have either."

"Don't upset yourself, Mama. Please. You must rest."

"I . . . must . . . talk."

I didn't argue. I knew she had something on her mind. I also knew, looking down at her horribly discolored face, that she could not live.

"Very well, Mama. What is it?"

"Miss Bingham and I talked. She would like you to remain at school. A language tutor to the girls. You spoke of seeking employment elsewhere. You must . . . not. Stay there in a good environment."

Her breathing was becoming labored, and her speech was growing more difficult to understand.

"I am pleased to hear that," I said softly. "We will both stay there."

"No, Nila. I am dying. Don't will me to live. That would be evil."

She was becoming irrational. "I want you with me, Mama. Your sister wants you to get well, and she asks your forgiveness."

"I will never forgive her. Never. Louis . . . Louis. . . ."

I didn't know if she was calling to him or talking about him. "What about Papa?" I asked.

"He should not have drowned."

Her head fell to one side.

"Mama!"

She was dead. I knew it, but kept calling to her, hoping to bring her back. The young intern came rushing in and pulled me free of her. I had gathered her in my arms and was crying uncontrollably. He pulled me to him and comforted me until I stopped sobbing.

Then I got my handkerchief from my purse and dried my tears. The intern had eased Mama's body flat on the bed. He closed her eyes and covered her face with the sheet.

"It probably won't help for me to tell you this now, as your loss is too great, but be grateful your mother is gone. She would have been completely helpless. The broken bones in her legs and arms would never have mended, not to mention the severe internal injuries."

Though I knew he spoke the truth, his words were small comfort. "What should I do now in regard to Mama?"

"Stop at the desk downstairs. They'll tell you what to do."

"Thank you, for comforting me, and for your kindness to Mama."

"That's why I'm here, Miss Parris. I am deeply sorry."

I went downstairs and was almost at the desk when my aunt came through the doorway. She knew without my saying a word that Mama was dead.

She hastened her step and took me in her arms. "I had a premonition shortly after you left. It's over, isn't it?"

I nodded. "I must go to the desk. They will tell me what to do."

"Please let me handle it, Nila."

"I appreciate your help, Auntie."

Dorothy Daniels

While I signed the papers releasing Mama's body to the mortician, my aunt telephoned Hanes Funeral Home and informed them that she would assume the cost of the funeral and would be there the following morning.

As we left the building, I remembered a small painting of Mama which Papa had done, and I told my aunt I would like the casket to remain closed, with the painting displayed on top. She liked the idea.

On the way back, Aunt Evelyn said she would feel more at ease if I remained with her at the hotel. She had already sent Francine, her personal maid, to my school with that message. I voiced no objection and was really glad I didn't have to return to the empty apartment.

"I keep the hotel suite reserved the entire year," my aunt informed me. "There is a second bedroom with a bath. I will buy a black dress for you. One can always have one's needs attended to at this hotel. When do you wish the funeral to be?"

"Tomorrow afternoon," I said. "Mama is dead. I must adjust to it."

"I hope you will come live with me now," my aunt said.

"No," I replied. "Mama did regain consciousness minutes before she died. She said Miss Bingham wished to hire me as a language tutor for her students."

"Would you like that?" my aunt asked.

"I am quite adept at languages," I told her.

"How many do you speak?"

"Five," I replied.

"So, you're a linguist," she said. "I'm proud of you, dear, but sorry you won't come back to Massachusetts with me."

"Please don't think I'm unappreciative, Auntie," I said. "I just don't think I would feel at home."

"Why not?" My aunt's astonishment was evident in her voice.

10

"Your wealth, for one thing," I said. "And I am already in your debt. I'm glad Mama didn't know you paid for my education."

"My dear," my aunt said, "you don't think the school officials would have paid your mama what they did and also have enrolled you as a student out of the goodness of their hearts?"

"That's exactly what Mama and I did think," I said.

"I'm sorry to have disillusioned you." She paused, then asked hesitantly, "Did you ask Loretta to forgive me?"

"I'll not lie to you, Auntie," I said, almost too weary to talk about it. "Mama said she didn't have a sister. When I pressed her, she said she would never forgive you."

"What else did she say?" my aunt asked softly. I knew she was hurt, but that she wanted to hear everything Mama had said.

"Not very much. She was near death. I told her we both wanted her to live. She said that to will her to live would be evil."

My aunt's features expressed shock. "Why would she say such a thing?"

"I don't know, other than that she was in great pain. The doctor said she would have been a helpless invalid had she lived."

"She'd have lacked nothing. I'd have seen to that. I loved her. I did an unforgivable thing in objecting to her marriage."

"Mama also said Papa was strong and should not have drowned."

"Perhaps he was," my aunt admitted. "I really didn't know him well."

"Auntie, I am grateful that I'm staying with you tonight."

"Tomorrow we will go to the mortician's. Then I'll drop you off at school."

"That is kind of you, Auntie."

"No more than suitable. Please remember, your mother was my sister. Despite what she thought, I loved her."

I rested my hand on my aunt's forearm. "I'm sure you did. Perhaps if Papa had lived, Mama might not have resented you so much."

Once in the suite, my aunt brought me directly to the softly lit second bedroom. The maid assigned to the floor had come in and turned down the beds. My aunt had left word to have a warm bath waiting for me. A beautiful silk nightdress lay across the foot of the bed. I undressed and got into the jasmine-scented water in the steaming tub. I gratefully stretched out full-length, relaxed, and began to feel very sleepy. Afterward, I dried off, slipped into the silk nightdress, and sank into bed, where I quickly fell asleep.

True to her word, my aunt had a suitable outfit for me—a black dress and a black hat with a filmy veil. Francine had laid these out before wakening me for my breakfast. But once I saw the black dress and accessories, my memory came back with a rush, and I had little appetite. Francine, however, was firm, following my aunt's orders that I eat in preparation for the long and difficult day.

I ate enough to satisfy her, then quickly dressed. To my amazement, the dress fit perfectly.

I looked in the mirror as I put on my hat and was surprised at my appearance. The haggard look I had last night was no longer evident. I was still pale, but my gray eyes were bright and alert. My hair was jet-black, my face oval, and my mouth was well-shaped, like Mama's had been.

My aunt was also dressed in black. We went together to the mortician's. The driver carried a large box inside. When I regarded it questioningly, my aunt said, "Clothing for Loretta."

"Thank you, Auntie. I completely forgot."

"You're young—too young to have to go through this. I will attend to everything. Please wait in the anteroom. I telephoned the mortician again last night after you retired to make certain he understood." My aunt paused, then added, "Oh, I almost forgot—Miss Bingham telephoned me this morning to say she wishes to attend the services. I will meet you both at the school this afternoon."

"Thank you for all you have done. I wonder what I would have done alone."

"You would have managed well," she replied. "Though I'm glad you didn't have to, especially since this happens to be your birthday."

"You knew that?" I asked in astonishment.

She nodded. "You're nineteen."

I thought of the cake I was to have shared with Mama. Instead, I was going to attend her funeral.

My aunt's arm closed around my shoulders. "I can imagine what you are thinking. Let your grief be tempered with the memory of what that doctor told you—your mother would not have wished to live an invalid's life."

"I know," I replied, fully aware of Mama's zest for life. "When we leave here, will you be coming with me to school?" I asked.

"No, my dear, I changed my mind. You have only a few hours to yourself until the two o'clock service. Your mama will be buried alongside your papa. The cemetery is close by, isn't it?"

"About a half-mile from the academy. Mama told me there are three graves in that plot."

"Yes, that's what Mr. Hanes said. I pray the third one will remain empty for a long time."

The funeral director, Mr. Hanes, was middle-aged and kindly. His manner was one befitting an undertaker, and after expressing his condolences, he assured us everything would be done in good taste.

Services would be conducted in the school chapel by

Reverend Beasley, who was the chaplain there. I knew that would have pleased Mama.

"After I have selected a casket," my aunt said, "I am going to return to my suite until it is time for the funeral. I have a headache from lack of sleep."

"I'm sorry, Auntie."

She eyed me carefully. "Are you afraid to be alone?"

"No. I don't know how to thank you. I am deeply grateful."

"There is no need for gratitude. My debt to you can never be repaid. Your mother couldn't forgive me. I hope you will."

"I do, Auntie," I assured her.

Mr. Hanes told my aunt he was ready to show her the caskets. My aunt stood up. "Please let me do this one thing alone, Nila. While I'm gone, you may open the box and see what I brought for Loretta to wear."

I went to the long table and opened the box. When I removed the tissue paper, I exclaimed aloud at the beaded gown with its high neck, long sleeves, and matching satin slippers. I lifted the bodice to see it better. Sunlight filtering through the curtained windows caught the multi-colored beads and sent sparkling shafts of light around the room. I noticed some feathers tucked among the tissue and was puzzled by their presence.

I replaced the gown in the box, and sat down. I felt lonely and lost, a feeling I would have to grow used to. Mama and I had had each other, but how lonely she must have been without Papa. I had observed those girls at the academy who had received their engagement rings upon graduation. Even though some weren't pretty, they were so filled with love that each one looked beautiful. I thoroughly believed that the love between a man and a woman must be the most fulfilling kind.

My aunt returned shortly with Mr. Hanes. She said,

"I hope you will approve of my choice, dear. I want you to have a beautiful memory of your mama."

"The gown is exquisite, Auntie, but the casket must be kept closed. Mama's face was swollen and discolored."

"Please don't upset yourself, Miss Parris," Mr. Hanes said. "I hire the services of a gentleman who performs miracles. He has seen your mother's features and has assured me that there will be no evidence of the terrible accident. Should there be, he will attach feathers on the sides of her hair which will conceal any facial scars."

I thought of the beautiful gown my aunt had purchased and relented.

"You may go now, Nila," my aunt said. "We will meet you at the funeral."

I thanked her again, went outside, and was helped into the carriage. The driver knew where the school was, so I settled back and closed my eyes.

It was a goodly drive back to Miss Bingham's Academy. When the driver pulled up before the building, I handed him a bill.

He refused it with a smile of apology, saying, "Couldn't take it, miss. Mrs. Dunbar takes good care of me. I take her wherever she wishes to go. Me an' my wife are beholden to her. Never forgets us on the holidays, either."

"Thank you for the safe ride," I replied. "I've been in some carriages and marveled that I got out alive."

He nodded. "I've seen 'em. Just want to say, miss, I read about the terrible accident that happened to your mother. I'm real sorry, miss. Real sorry."

He was a middle-aged gentleman with a heavy crop of whiskers, and he was wearing the proper spotless attire. He helped me alight, removed his derby hat, and bowed.

"I will tell my aunt how considerate you were."

"Thank you, miss. I'd appreciate that."

I went up the stairs and passed through the rooms reserved for the students' visitors—either family or gentlemen friends. Mama's duty was to chaperone them and to look after their needs. I knew everyone would miss her.

Our suite was halfway down the corridor. The sitting room was furnished in wicker, with bright, flowered cushions. The paintings on the walls had been done by Papa. He had had a better than average talent, but was not really a professional.

I sat down in a chair and regarded Papa's small painting of Mama. Three days ago she had sat across from me as we discussed our plans for the summer. That was the day of her fatal accident. Today, we were to have celebrated my birthday.

My musings were interrupted by a light tap on the door. Miss Bingham embraced me when I opened the door and expressed her sympathy over the horrible tragedy. Her features were plain. She favored brown dresses with plain bodices, high lace collars, and deep-pleated skirts. She walked with a cane, though no one ever knew why, since her posture was ramrod straight. She walked briskly, without a trace of a limp.

"Your mother will be deeply missed, Nila. She was loved by everyone."

I thanked her, motioned her to the chair Mama usually sat in, and resumed my seat.

She continued, "I came, not only to express my sympathy, but to tell you that my housekeeper took a message that Mrs. Dunbar will be unable to attend the services."

"What happened?" I asked in alarm.

"She collapsed at the funeral home."

I stood up quickly. "I must go there."

Miss Bingham raised a restraining hand. "No, my dear. She regained consciousness and is on her way back to the hotel. She asked your forgiveness and understanding."

House of Silence

"She was Mama's sister." I pressed my fingers to my brow, distraught. "But then, you know that."

She nodded. "I wrote letters once a month informing her of your welfare, and your mother's. I hope you bear me no grudge for indulging in deception."

"I had no idea—and neither did Mama—that our lodging and my tuition were being paid for."

"That was the agreement, Nila," Miss Bingham said kindly. "Our employees do not receive high wages, but they have the prestige of teaching here, and live in pleasant surroundings."

"Beautiful surroundings," I said.

"Which cost a great deal. I will accept only the daughters of well-known families who are, of course, financially sound."

I couldn't help but smile. "What you are really saying, Miss Bingham, is that this is a very snobbish school."

"No," she chided me. "You said that."

"Tell me, would you have hired Mama, given me free tuition, and allowed us this comfortable suite if it hadn't been for my aunt?"

Her face reddened, and she looked down at her hands, clasped in her lap. "I couldn't have afforded to, Nila."

"I think you could have easily with the high tuition fees here."

"Very well." She sighed and raised her eyes. "I will put it bluntly. This is not a charitable institution."

This time my face colored. "Mama said that you would like to hire me as a tutor for the students now that I have graduated."

Once again she looked uncomfortable. "That was before the accident. Your aunt had instructed that you and your mama be given every consideration here."

"Am I still not to be given every consideration? Can I not make it on my own merits instead of on my aunt's money? I don't expect a suite this size. One room would do nicely."

"Our instructors, and even our tutors, have all had a much higher education than you."

"But I am an accomplished linguist. I speak five languages fluently and am in the process of learning three others."

"Suppose you discuss your remaining here with your aunt." She stood up, her discomfiture quite obvious.

"Did my aunt terminate her donations to the academy?" I asked.

"I don't know. It was my understanding that you would return to her home in Massachusetts. I know she wants that very much."

"She offered it. But Mama wanted me to remain here. And I would like to. I'm certain I would not be a disappointment to you."

"We have standards of education. While your mama was alive and your aunt was providing most generously for both of you, I was willing to break a few rules. You are much too young to be a housemother, and that is what this cottage must have. Someone must replace your mama."

"I understand," I said.

"Of course," she went on in a hesitant manner, "if your aunt still wishes to include the academy among her philanthropies, I will give serious thought to hiring you."

"I wouldn't want my remaining here to be contingent on my aunt's generosity," I said.

"It isn't as if I were pushing you out onto the street," she said hurriedly. "You do have a wealthy aunt who will see to it that you never want for anything."

"I am young, also, and certain I can find suitable employment."

"If that is your preference, I will give you an excellent reference. You would make a fine governess."

House of Silence

I already sensed the loneliness of such an occupation. "I will check the advertisements after the funeral service. I understand, by the way, that you wish to attend."

Once again she apologized. "In view of this little talk we've had, I would feel too uncomfortable there."

"I understand." And I did. I had learned a lot in the last twenty-four hours. I was grateful Mama never knew that she was beholden to her sister for her livelihood and my education. Strangely enough, I felt no resentment toward my aunt, and knowing Mama's sweet nature, I was puzzled that—even though she knew she was near death—she would never forgive her sister.

And so I was the sole mourner at Mama's funeral. After the service, Reverend Beasley offered his condolences and accompanied me to the gravesite.

I refused to think about what I would do with my life until after the ceremony. I thanked Mr. Hanes for the splendid work done on Mama's face. She looked beautiful with the feathers in her hair, touching her cheeks and hiding all discoloration. She looked as if she were just sleeping. The gown was exquisite—a pity she'd never had anything that beautiful in life.

To my surprise, Miss Bingham was waiting for me in my suite. She told me that my aunt had telephoned and assured her that my salary for tutoring would be taken care of and I was to continue to have the suite I had shared with Mama. She added that my aunt had also stated that, should I change my mind, I need only call her.

"Do you remember that you said you would feel uncomfortable attending Mama's services after our little talk? Well, I would feel uncomfortable remaining here. May I use your telephone to inform my aunt that I would be very grateful to visit her for a while?"

To my surprise, Miss Bingham looked disappointed, but remained poised. "I will be pleased to call her for you. Your aunt said that she would be here at seven in the morning. That gives you only a few hours for packing. Do try to get a good night's rest."

"Thank you, Miss Bingham. And thank you for keeping my aunt's secret all these years."

"In case you have forgotten, Nila, that was your aunt's arrangement. Good-bye, my dear, and good luck."

She extended a hand, which I grasped briefly. I felt no resentment toward the woman.

She went to the door and turned. "You know, Nila, I am glad you are leaving, for you would be lonely here. I might add, it would be profitable for me if you stayed. Your aunt said she would contribute more than ever. Her main consideration was your happiness."

"That is good to hear, Miss Bingham. Thank you. Please tell my aunt I will be ready. Oh—I don't know what to do about my trunk."

"She told me to see that it be shipped to her home in Massachusetts."

I'd thought I would burst into tears once the door closed. Instead, I smiled. For some strange reason, I wanted to be with Aunt Evelyn. After all, she was Mama's sister, and like me, she had no one.

I went into the bedroom to pack Mama's trunk. I would need to take only Papa's paintings and the few knick-knacks we had accumulated. I would leave Mama's clothes here with a note on them stating that they were to be given to Reverend Beasley for those in need. I finished my chore after midnight and was weary. Even so, the empty bed alongside mine made the horror of what had happened to Mama flash through my mind.

TWO

My aunt informed me that it would be a two-hour ride to her home after we changed trains in Beaverville. It was beautiful country, and I only wished Mama could have been with me. My aunt's pleasure at my decision to come with her helped relieve my sadness and feelings of loneliness. At such a time, it was good to be wanted.

The train finally pulled into the station. There were a good number of people on the opposite platform. As I observed the passengers, a small dog jumped down between the tracks. A lady called frantically for him to come back to her. She started to step down onto the ties to retrieve the dog, but a gentleman pulled her back.

A moment later we heard the shrill whistle of a train. The dog would be killed if he didn't get out of the locomotive's path. Everyone was calling to the animal, who paid no heed to his danger. Without thinking, I stuck my head out the window and commanded the dog to jump back on the platform. He turned his head to look at me. I repeated my command, and he obeyed instantly.

Francine exclaimed, "He obeyed you, mademoiselle."

"Indeed he did, and just in time, too," my aunt added. "I'm astonished."

"So am I," I said numbly.

Our train stopped, and we walked down the aisle.

Dorothy Daniels

To my surprise, the gentleman who had transported me to Bellevue Hospital awaited us.

My aunt explained, "I decided to bring Pierce and Dulcy Lavery back here. They were tired of New York City, so it worked out very well. Pierce, our baggage is on the rack inside. We are going to cross the tracks to see the dog."

My aunt led the way. People on the opposite platform were already boarding. When we reached the end of the platform, the lady, who now had a strong hold on the leash, called out a greeting as she walked toward us. Suddenly, the dog stopped so rapidly in front of her that she stumbled, but quickly regained her balance.

The dog looked directly at me, bared his teeth, and backed away, snarling. His mistress spoke sharply to him and tried to urge him toward us, but he wouldn't move.

"I'm so sorry," she said as we moved closer to her. "And I'm truly grateful to you, miss, for rescuing my pet. He'd have been killed if it hadn't been for you."

The dog snarled more vehemently and attracted the attention of the passengers. Heads stuck out of every window facing the platform.

I said, "It's obvious he doesn't like me. You'd better board your train."

The conductor called a warning to her as the engineer blew the train whistle for departure. She was distraught and hesitant to leave us.

"My niece is right," my aunt said. "Please get on the train. After all, we are strangers, and it's quite natural for your dog to resent us."

"He has never resented anyone." She was on the verge of tears. "He's a gentle and loving dog."

"You'll miss your train if you don't get aboard," I said. "We understand."

She nodded briefly and turned back to her pet. To my amazement, the dog once again became a placid

House of Silence

animal. I gave my aunt a surprised look, which she returned with one of understanding. Pierce and Francine came into view, carrying our luggage.

Before boarding, the woman picked up the dog. She called a farewell to us. The dog had thrust his nose under her arm as if he couldn't bear the sight of me.

My aunt urged me off the platform, and we walked to our carriage. The horses were beautiful and so was the vehicle, which was covered in lavish dark-green satin. The nap on the carpeted floor was so thick the toes of my shoes disappeared in it.

"I don't believe I've ever ridden in anything so elegant," I said. "I'm just beginning to realize how lucky I am."

"I'm the lucky one, my dear," my aunt said. "I only hope you will stay."

"If I am as unpopular with the natives as I was with that little dog, you probably won't want me to stay."

"Nonsense," she replied sternly. "It was a most ungrateful little animal. But then, it *was* an animal. No human would treat you in such a fashion."

"At least a human doesn't growl or snarl," I said. We all laughed, and I lost the embarrassment I had felt standing there in front of so many bystanders.

"Just remember," my aunt said kindly, "your embarrassment was no greater than that of the dog's owner. I was proud of you. Everyone on that platform not only admired you, but was astonished that the dog obeyed your command when he wouldn't listen to anybody else."

There was no time for further talk, as we turned off the dirt road and entered a drive leading to a house which could only be called a mansion.

"My dear," my aunt said, "you haven't spoken a word since we left the depot. Are you having regrets?"

I quickly reassured her. "I was enchanted by the countryside. Here and there I caught a glimpse of ivy-covered houses."

She looked pleased. "Is such landscape new to you?"

I nodded. "Mama and I could never afford a vacation, although during the summer we often took one-day excursions."

She sobered. "You made the most of what little you had."

"We were rich with happiness, Auntie. Mama had a wonderful sense of humor. And during the summer, she gave me all the attention she had to devote exclusively to the students during the semester."

"I am sure they loved her."

"Yes." Then I commented on our surroundings, "I can scarcely believe my eyes. Your mansion is beautiful there at the top of the hill. I'm not certain I will be comfortable in such luxury."

"I hope you will like it," she said. "One day it will be yours."

"It's too luxurious for me. I hope you live a long life so you will be able to enjoy it for many years."

"A gentleman, Giles Lazarno, lives in the house also," my aunt said. "He was a dear friend of my late husband, Charles. Giles makes himself useful in many ways. As the result of bad investments he is penniless. When Giles fell ill, Charles brought him here and asked that he remain. He recovered, but my poor Charles suffered a heart attack ten years ago."

"Mr. Lazarno must be a comfort to you."

"He is most helpful and gracious. His presence will make it less lonely for you when I take to my suite with severe headaches. My attorney, Peter Rogerson, also comes here from time to time. My extensive holdings throughout the United States necessitate his frequent visits from Boston. He is no more than thirty. I know you will like him."

"I hope he likes me," I said.

"He will." She spoke with quiet assurance. "He has been with the firm only a short time, but has already become extremely successful and has acquired something of a fortune."

"If you have such extensive holdings, he must be in a good position to know how to invest his own money."

"True," my aunt agreed. "Though I believe he would be a success no matter what he aspired to. Well, we've reached the top of the drive. Just remember, Nila, if you are the least bit unhappy, come to me."

I said, "I would be most ungrateful if I were unhappy here."

"You have no idea how pleased I am." My aunt smiled hesitantly. "I was desolate when you told me you wished to tutor at the academy. When Miss Bingham called yesterday afternoon to tell me of your decision, I was overcome with happiness."

"I must be honest, Auntie," I said. "If she had kept her word, I would not have come. I have nowhere else to go."

"I should have talked with her," my aunt said, "but I didn't know of her conversation with Loretta. Had I known that it was what you wished, there would have been no need for her to have said what she did."

"Did she tell you?" I asked in surprise.

"I questioned her when she called, and I fear I was a little abrupt. I will apologize to her. Enough talk for now. Pierce has been patiently waiting to help us down."

"Glad to, Mrs. Dunbar," he said politely.

My aunt smiled down at him. "I'm glad I had the good sense to ask you and Dulcy to come here. I was very pleased with the interview last night. Of course, I've known you for years."

He spoke as he helped us down. "Dulcy's happy about it too, ma'am. I'll bring the baggage in, an' Francine can show me where to put it."

"I instructed Miss Bingham to send your trunk immediately," my aunt said.

"Thank you, Auntie. Other than my clothes, I have only a few mementos."

"I intend to replenish your wardrobe," my aunt said. "In fact, the black dress fit you so perfectly that I have ordered another in beige."

"I wish you hadn't. You've done too much already."

"I have only begun." She placed her arm about my waist as we approached the magnificent entrance. We walked through the marble entrance with its thick, round columns that supported the second-story porch.

First I was introduced to Dulcy, who stood in the enormous entrance hall awaiting us. She was buxom but trim, with iron-gray hair coiled about her head, and wore a black uniform with a white apron. Her dark eyes observed me politely as she curtsied. My aunt introduced us, then asked where Mr. Lazarno was.

"He went into the village, ma'am," Dulcy said. "Said he hoped to be back before you arrived."

My aunt turned to me. "You can meet him at dinner. Just now I want to get cleaned up."

Francine had been hovering in the hall, awaiting orders from her mistress.

My aunt addressed her. "Please fill our tubs. Then you may attend to your own toilette."

"Thank you, madame," she said, flashing me a smile. I liked her. I doubted she was more than twenty-five.

Dulcy said, "Mr. Lazarno had two ladies come today from the village to do the cleaning. They filled the tubs when they saw the carriage turn in the drive."

"Good," my aunt said. "I must compliment Giles on being able to get help from the village."

"He said they are working at the hotel, but that this was their day off, and they didn't turn up their noses at a chance to make extra money."

"I'm happy you and Pierce came, also."

"We're the lucky ones," she said. "If you'll excuse

me, ma'am, I'll go back to the kitchen. Got my cookin' to do."

The stairway was wide and carpeted. An enormous crystal chandelier caught the rays of the afternoon sun.

At the top of the stairs, my aunt paused and said, "The house has three wings. My suite is in the center wing. You will have a suite at the left end. Giles's suite is at the right end."

I was astonished at the size of the house. We were standing directly in front of the center wing. Most of the doors were closed, allowing little light to slip through, so I could not see how far the hall extended. Francine and Pierce had followed us up the stairway.

"You may go with Francine," my aunt said. "She will see you to your suite. I hope you like it."

I smiled reassuringly and followed Francine. The hallway was wide, and large paintings and tapestries covered the walls. It was like living in a museum.

I followed Francine along the left corridor, wondering why my aunt hadn't chosen it instead of the dark, dismal center wing. Windows lined one side, letting in the late afternoon sun. Near the end, Francine opened a door and stepped back.

"This is your suite, mademoiselle," she said with a warm smile. "I am pleased madame wished you to live here. It is so pretty, and furnished for someone young and lovely like you."

"Thank you, Francine," I said.

She was right. The sitting room had a large fireplace and a chintz covered settee with matching chairs in bright flowered fabrics. Several small tables with attractive knick-knacks on them sat beside the chairs.

I went over, looked out the window, and was presented with a beautiful view of the garden. "It's like a fairyland," I said, turning to Francine.

"Oui," she replied. "Come into the bedroom, please. It is also pretty."

The bed had a ruffled white organdy spread lined

with pink satin. There was a matching dressing table, dresser, and a tall chest with teakwood drawers. The rug was a soft gray, and a full-length triple mirror stood in one corner, reflecting the entire room.

"I can't believe this is real," I said to Francine, who was eyeing me with amusement.

"It is, mademoiselle. The bath is the door behind you. In a few days, your dresses, gowns, hats, gloves, and undergarments will arrive. I'll unpack them for you, and I'll be glad to make the selections. I hope you'll let me help you."

"Did you select the black suit I am wearing?"

"*Oui,* mademoiselle."

"In that case, you needn't have the slightest doubt. You know, I hadn't intended to remain here very long. I still don't, though it won't be easy to leave such luxury."

"Oh, mademoiselle, I hope you'll stay. It is so good to have someone young in the house."

"Thank you, Francine. It is good for me to have someone like you to talk to."

She smiled her thanks, started to leave, then turned back. "Oh, mademoiselle, I almost forgot. Your aunt always dresses for dinner. Even when she eats alone. Usually, though, Monsieur Giles eats with her. He is a very gracious gentleman. You will like him."

"I don't have an expensive gown," I said. "But I believe I have something that will do, though it doesn't seem proper so soon after Mama's death."

"I think your mother would not like you to wear black," Francine said seriously. "You are young. You must enjoy life, even though it's difficult."

"I know," I said. "I'll give it some thought."

"You have time to rest a little after you bathe. Dinner is at seven. You wish me to unpack your bags?"

"No, thank you. I can manage."

She closed the door softly behind her, and I found the ensuing silence depressing. I tried to remember the beauty that surrounded me, but it made no difference. I was in a strange place, and I felt lost and lonely. It would take me a long time to get over Mama's tragic death. I thought of the suite of rooms we had shared through the years, and realized I would have been far more lonely there. Besides, we had lived at the school only through the generosity of my aunt. The more I thought about it, the less I liked Miss Bingham. She had tolerated us only because of my aunt's money.

I unpacked my bags and prepared for my bath.

I surveyed myself in the triple mirror and had to admit the brief nap had brought a glow to my cheeks.

My frock was simple, with a high neck, leg-o'-mutton sleeves, and a wide satin waistband, which showed off my small waist. The skirt and bodice were made of crepe silk. I was not in the mood to wear jewelry. I had dressed for dinner, as was the custom in this house, but I would not "gild the lily," so to speak.

At five minutes to seven, I left for the dining room. I had no idea where it was, but I knew someone would be downstairs to direct me there.

I was right. I descended the stairs partway and paused once again to admire the beautiful crystal chandelier.

"Ah, Miss Nila Parris." I looked for the source of the masculine voice and gaped in awe.

"What is it, my dear?" the gentleman asked, smiling at my astonished face.

I stammered my reply. "I didn't expect to see—I mean, I wasn't prepared for anyone so handsome."

He nodded graciously and said, "Thank you."

His features seemed carved out of granite; his eyes were icy blue; his chin strong; and his skin was bronzed from the sun—making him appear even more handsome. His manner was so self-assured, one could assume he was the epitome of success.

He offered me his arm. "We will dine alone. Your

aunt has one of her severe headaches and must lie in absolute darkness."

"Do you think she would like me to visit her after dinner?"

"I hate to have to tell you, but she wants complete silence. It's why she loves it here."

"I noticed how quiet the house was after Francine left me."

"The rugs are thickly piled, the draperies lined, and the furniture heavily upholstered. She has done it deliberately."

"Is it because of her headaches?"

"Yes. She has traveled all over the world seeking a cure. Nothing has helped. She has consulted learned men of medicine and a few quacks. It's a horrible illness for one who has done so much good."

"I know all she has done for Mama and me," I said.

"I am living here on her bounty," he admitted. "I should be ashamed to tell you, but I insist anyone who comes here knows."

"I am sure you repay my aunt with your company, and I suppose you are her escort at social events."

His eyes regarded me kindly. "You're a smart young lady."

"I hope to repay her for her kindness."

He patted my hand. "I'm sure you will."

"I don't know how it would be possible," I said.

"One day the answer will come," he said. "It might even come from her."

"You make it sound very mysterious," I said.

"Perhaps it will be a secret trust which she will hand down to you."

"Now I *am* puzzled," I said.

"We'll forget it and eat our dinner."

Art objects hung in the hall, which was well-lit with beautiful hand-painted lamps. Light from rooms on our left drifted into the hallway.

Mr. Lazarno said, "The library, the music room, and

House of Silence

the ballroom are on this side of the house. The other side has parlors and rooms which hold treasures from all over the world. Your aunt and uncle traveled everywhere. When he died, she lost interest in travel—unless she'd heard of some medicine man who might be able to help her."

Then he informed me that he and Francine accompanied her. "It would be unseemly," he concluded, "to do otherwise."

We had finally reached the luxurious dining room. The room was paneled, and twin Tiffany lamps hung from the ceiling, their exquisite colors sending a glow around the room.

"It seems ridiculous for us to dine at such a large table, but your aunt is a great one for formality."

"Are all meals eaten here?"

Mr. Lazarno said, "No, just dinner. There is a small dining room with a beautiful view looking out onto a lake. It is ideal during the winter, with its two small fireplaces. I see to it that there are plenty of logs and keep trim splitting wood."

Mr. Lazarno seated me at the head of the table. When I hesitated, he said, "Please sit down, Miss Parris. Your aunt sent word through Francine that she wished you to sit at the head of the table. After all, one day you will."

"I don't like to think that way," I said uncomfortably.

"Relax, my dear," he replied in his courtly manner. "It will please your aunt."

"Would she be angry if I refused?" I asked as I seated myself.

He moved to my right and sat down. "No. Just hurt."

He rang the bell, and to my amazement, Pierce entered, dressed in a butler's uniform.

He poured wine into sparkling crystal glasses. While

31

Pierce filled our soup plates, Mr. Lazarno turned his attention to me.

"Tell me a little about yourself," he said.

"I daresay that, since you have lived with my aunt, you must know a great deal about me."

"Yes," he admitted. "Your aunt was concerned about your Mama's life-style. She loved Loretta, and she wanted to love you."

"Suppose you tell me about your life," I said. "I'm certain it is far more exciting than mine."

"When I was young," he said, "I lived in New York City and enjoyed life."

"Would you like to live there now?" I asked.

"No, I'm very happy here."

"Is it always this quiet?"

"What do you mean?"

"Doesn't my aunt entertain?"

"Hasn't she spoken with you about that?"

I waited until Pierce had finished serving our soup and left the room.

"Spoken with me about what?" I asked.

"The village."

"Not a word."

"She is very generous with those people, yet they will not accept her."

"Why not?" I asked.

"I'd prefer that she tell you." He lifted his glass. "Let us drink to your future."

We toasted each other and smiled. I then commented on the soup, which was delicious.

"I believe you will find Dulcy's cooking excellent," said Giles. "She and Pierce worked for Mrs. Dunbar when she was in New York as you know, and just arrived here last night. They both wanted to work in the country, and we have taken them on. It's a blessing for Evelyn. Now she'll have no worries about this big house being kept up. And if I can persuade the young ladies who work at the hotel in the summer to continue to work here on their days off, her troubles will be over."

"I didn't see the village," I said.

"It is on the other side of the depot. You will see it. The natives are not always friendly, but you have a sweet way about you which they should find appealing."

"I hope more so than the little dog at the depot."

He eyed me curiously. "I didn't hear anything about it."

I related the embarrassing incident while Pierce removed our soup plates and served our main course.

When I finished, Giles said, "That is very interesting."

"I wish it had never happened. I almost wish I hadn't commanded the little dog to jump back on the platform."

"You don't mean that. After all, you saved its life."

"Yes," I admitted. "But it was almost as if I couldn't help myself. The words just came from my mouth."

He laughed. "He was an ungrateful little mutt, wasn't he?"

I frowned. "I think he was afraid of me."

"Was the animal really small?"

I managed a smile. "A little poodle. Either he feared me or disliked me."

"That *is* puzzling. What did your aunt say?"

"She was proud of me."

His hearty laughter cut through the ominous quiet that seemed to have filled the room. I was glad Mr. Giles Lazarno lived here. I could well understand my aunt's wishing him to remain.

"Let us go into the study," he said. "You may have your coffee, and I will sip brandy. That is usually what your aunt and I do."

"I would like to see the study, as well as the rest of the house and the village."

"The house you can explore at your leisure," he said. "I will tell you about the village."

We entered the study. This room was charming, with its books, paintings, and burgundy velvet draperies. The fireplace glowed with cheer and welcoming warmth. The coffee service was already in the room, and Mr. Lazarno poured me a cup. Then he picked up the decanter of brandy and poured a generous quantity into his glass.

"You may think it strange to use the fireplaces in the summer," he said, taking a seat opposite me. "But the walls are very thick to ensure coolness in hot weather and warmth in cold."

"I think it's delightful. I wish you would tell me about the village."

"It's like most New England villages. The old hotel there is always crammed with summer visitors. The Arneil family owns it, and they are about to build a new one on the other side of the lake. I fear your aunt didn't make any friends when she opposed it."

"Why should she object to it?" I asked.

"She likes quiet. If she had wanted to make certain no one would purchase the property, she should have bought it herself."

"Who are the Arneils?" I asked.

"They are from Boston." He cupped the brandy snifter in his hand. "Charming people. In fact, your aunt got along very well with them until they purchased that land. She'll get over it."

"It does seem a shame that such a beautiful lake isn't enjoyed by people."

"Oh, they enjoy it now. But it's a fair distance from the village, whereas once the hotel is constructed, they will just need to walk out the door. Once it is built, private dwellings will follow. It always happens that way."

"She might grow to like it," I said.

He took a sip of his brandy before replying. "I

wouldn't wager a bet on it. She gets dreadful headaches when she becomes upset or fatigued."

"I feel responsible for her tiredness," I said. "She assumed all the responsibility for Mama's funeral."

"You did her a favor, really, by making her feel useful. Part of her trouble is that she has too much time on her hands. I'm as grateful for your coming as she is."

"Thank you, Mr. Lazarno." I set my cup and saucer on the table. "I hope you will forgive me, but I am tired and would like to be excused."

He stood up. "I haven't had time to tell you about the village, but that can wait."

"Perhaps I could go there tomorrow," I said.

"An excellent idea," he exclaimed. "If Evelyn feels up to it, she might take you to lunch at the Arneil Inn."

"I shan't expect her to do that," I said.

"If she doesn't feel up to it, I will take you."

"Thank you. I would be most grateful."

He again offered his arm and accompanied me to the foot of the stairway. "Is there anything you need? If you are afraid to move about this large place alone, I'll go with you upstairs."

"That won't be necessary," I said. "I'm beginning to feel quite at home, thanks to you. It was a most pleasant evening."

"Thank you, my dear. Sleep well."

When I reached the top of the stairs, I looked down. He was still standing there, a half-smile on his handsome face. "You're a very beautiful young lady, Nila. You made this old fellow feel rather important tonight."

"You're not old, Mr. Lazarno."

"Fifty isn't young."

I went to my suite. The lights were already burning, and my bed was turned down. I extinguished the lamps in the sitting room and got ready for bed. I felt a sense of guilt for being so contented, but I knew Mama would have understood. If it hadn't been for my aunt, I don't know what I would have done. I wondered if I would have qualified for a position as governess, though I supposed, having learned the social graces and having been a good student, I would have had little trouble in finding a position.

I blew out the lamps in the bedroom and stood waiting for my eyes to adjust to the darkness. It only took a few moments, and to my delight, I found the room flooded with moonlight.

I went to one of the large window seats. I was just about to open the window when I was startled by an elongated shadow. I thought it might be Mr. Lazarno taking a stroll before retiring, but I was wrong. The figure that came into view was slender, with hair falling well below her shoulders. She was wearing a black robe of some kind. I couldn't identify her from the back. A great deal of shrubbery hid her from view as she crossed the lawn.

I was tempted to open the window and call out a greeting, but I didn't want to startle anyone. The slenderness of the figure reminded me of Francine, yet what would she be doing wandering about the estate in darkness?

There was a mild breeze which caught her robe and made it billow. She did not attempt to straighten it. She passed through an open area, and though she was moving farther away from the house, I strained my eyes to see if I could identify her. I knew the full moon would illuminate her if she turned around.

She was passing alongside more shrubbery just as the fickle breeze caught at the robe, and raised it so high that the hem caught on a branch. She was moving just fast enough to slip free of the robe. I exclaimed aloud in surprise, for I could see that she was completely nude.

To my dismay, I was now able to see her face and

realized it was Francine. She freed the robe from the branches and slipped it back on, holding her hands in front of her to prevent the same thing from happening again. At least that is what I assumed. She quickened her pace and entered the formal garden, disappearing from view as she entered the arbor. I might have pursued her had I believed she was sleepwalking, but she seemed to be in full possession of her senses.

Yet where could she be going at this hour of the night? I had assumed she was a respectable young lady. Could it be she was headed for a romantic rendezvous? I found it hard to believe, for I was of the opinion my aunt owned most of the property around here, and I doubted that anything went on which she did not know about. If she had suspected Francine of carrying on a clandestine affair, I felt certain she would have dismissed her.

I warned myself not to condemn Francine. From the briskness of her pace, she seemed to have a definite destination. To swim in the lake—nude? I couldn't make myself believe that.

I left the window seat and got into bed, but it was impossible to shut out what I had seen. I couldn't discuss it with my aunt, especially if Francine was indulging in a liaison with a gentleman. Yet I couldn't dispel the feeling of uneasiness which gripped me. Even if Francine believed no one saw her, why would she go out wearing only a cloak over her body? The thought came that there *was* one thing I could do. I decided to explore the area behind the house, near the formal garden. There might be a path through the forest that led to some sort of dwelling. It seemed unlikely—but possible.

I thought of Mama and the seemingly careless accident she had had, which had resulted in her death. I still couldn't figure out an answer to that—or to the mystery of the little dog who had obeyed my command and then snarled at me. And now Francine's unusual behavior. Or was it unusual only to me? I knew I must keep quiet, yet I felt I had to investigate. I had no reason to think less of her, but my suspicions had been aroused. If only there were someone I could talk to. I felt as desolate and lonely as I had when I returned to school after Mama's burial. I felt the need to get out of the house. If possible, I would ask my aunt to take me to the village.

THREE

Francine was waiting at the foot of the stairs and told me that my aunt, having completely recovered from her headache, was in the small dining room.

"She is anxious to see you, mademoiselle," she said.

"I'm pleased she is well again," I said.

"It was fatigue. She has to be careful. Her blood pressure is too high, and when she gets excited or unhappy, it is likely to affect her badly."

"I'll remember that."

Francine directed me to the breakfast room, with its French doors opening onto a terrace. A sweep of lawn led down to the lake, which was sparkling in the sunlight. Directly across the lake was the spot where the hotel would be built, and I could understand my aunt's dismay at having the large grove of pines cut down in order to build an inn.

She greeted me with a smile. I bent and kissed her cheek.

"My dear, I suggest we lunch at the Arneil Inn. It will give you a chance to see the village and also to get acquainted with the Arneils."

"Are you friendly with them?" I asked in surprise.

She laughed. "Giles has been gossiping."

"Nothing unfavorable, Auntie."

"Good. You'll find ham, eggs, fruit, rolls, and coffee on the serving table.

"It's a lovely room." I spoke as I served myself. My aunt had already eaten and was sipping coffee. "I can see why you objected to the new hotel being built."

"I was wrong," she said quietly. "One cannot and should not stop progress."

We were rewarded with another beautiful day. We took a more scenic route into town—a wide brook flowed on one side, and along its banks were weeping willows. We passed one lovely house, and saw lambs grazing on the front lawn. This time my aunt didn't question my silence. She knew I was enthralled by all I saw.

The village was like many others. Everything was freshly painted. Stores lined the side of the village green opposite the Arneil Inn. The inn was an enormous white building with green shutters framing its many windows, and a porch that extended around all four sides. Green awnings and huge elms shaded the porch. There were rocking chairs with matching green seats and cushions. People were sunning themselves and playing backgammon.

The inn was across from a raised bandstand, and the guests could enjoy the music. My aunt told me that extra chairs were put out on the veranda at such times, and the overflow sat on the lawn.

When we entered the lobby, a middle-aged couple approached us. The lady was most attractive in her pink lace dress, and the gentleman had a kindly face. Both smiled a welcome as the lady extended her hand to my aunt.

"Thank you for honoring us with your presence, Evelyn," she said. "We have missed you."

"Giles brought me to my senses," my aunt replied. "Pearl, I want you and Andrew to meet my niece, Nila Parris. Nila, these two charming people are Mr. and Mrs. Arneil."

Mrs. Arneil, with her gracious manner, reminded me of Mama. "How delightful to meet you. I hope you have come for lunch."

"We have indeed," my aunt said.

"Then we must see that you get a choice table," Mr. Arneil said. "You are to be our guests."

"We don't expect that, Andrew," my aunt said. "We have no reservation."

"Neither Evelyn Dunbar nor her niece ever needs a reservation," he said, flashing me a smile. "We have too few young people here."

My aunt reached out and caught Mrs. Arneil's arm. "Pearl, before we go into the dining room, I would like to say something. I know I behaved terribly about the new inn. As you know, I had Peter Rogerson do everything possible to prevent it. I was wrong. I am very sorry for causing you such delay."

Mrs. Arneil smiled reassurance. "I'm sorry that for a little while we weren't the friends we have been. However, it's over now, and I am happy our friendship has been renewed."

"So am I," Mr. Arneil said.

"I'm happy you both have forgiven me," my aunt said. "My weakness has always been my stubborn nature. I have another reason to be thankful now that my niece is with me."

Mrs. Arneil said, "She will be a charming asset to your lovely home."

"Her mother, who was my sister, had a fatal accident five days ago in New York City," my aunt went on. "I persuaded Nila to visit for a while. I'm hoping she will like it so much she'll stay."

Mrs. Arneil rested her hands lightly on my shoulders. "Your aunt needs you, Nila. Try to get her out more. She has become very reclusive these past several years."

"I will do my best," I said quietly.

"I'm sorry about your mama, dear," Mrs. Arneil said, then turned to my aunt. "You must keep her occupied. We read about Mrs. Parris's accident. Horrible."

Mr. Arneil motioned us inside, saying, "Come, ladies, I will escort you to a table."

The dining room was enormous and quite attractive. It was divided into several sections, separated by artificial palms. Each section had a different color scheme. Despite the fact that it was nearly filled, the sound of voices was muted—the rug softened the noise. The ceiling was painted with pastoral scenes, and large mirrored posts supported the ceiling. It must have been elegant at night with the lights reflecting in them.

Mr. Arneil led us to a table in an alcove. Partially cut off from the rest of the room by the potted palms, we had complete privacy. The window beside our table looked out on the lawn, where a few guests were engaged in a game of croquet.

Mr. Arneil had provided each of us with a menu, and we decided on an omelette. We sat there at least fifteen minutes before our order was taken. It might have been longer if the young man seated alone at a nearby table hadn't noticed us craning our necks, trying to get the attention of any waiter who happened by.

He set his napkin on the table and cleared his throat. I felt him eyeing us both a little more than was necessary. My aunt's back was to him, so I made no mention of the fact that I thought he might come to our assistance.

Perhaps he did, for a waiter soon approached our table. There was no courteous greeting or friendly glance. He kept his eyes lowered to his order pad. My aunt seemed not to notice and ordered. He returned shortly with a pitcher of water and filled our glasses so carelessly that the contents spilled over the tops.

"Please be a little more careful, young man," my aunt said coldly.

"You're lucky I came to your table," was his tart reply.

I was annoyed by his rudeness and said, "Be careful you don't trip and soak one of the guests with the pitcher of water. You have such a sour disposition, anything could happen."

House of Silence

He sneered. "What're you doin', puttin' a curse on me?"

"Perhaps someone should," I replied, managing a smile, "before you destroy the reputation of this dining room."

He was about to say something, but instead turned away. He hadn't taken more than a few steps when he tripped, and the pitcher flew from his hand, spilling its contents and soaking a middle-aged lady seated a few tables away from us. The pitcher landed on his head and broke.

For a few moments, there was near pandemonium. The lady soaked with water screamed. The waiter had fallen against a tray laden with dishes and knocked that to the floor, covering the rug with food.

The young man I had observed at the nearby table moments before bent over the unconscious waiter.

I got up to see if I could help, but my aunt begged me to resume my seat. I did so, for I could see that other waiters had arrived and lifted the unconscious waiter and were carrying him out of the room. The young gentleman was talking quietly and earnestly to some guests at the next table, who nodded understandingly.

He went next to the guest who had been soaked with water. She was already on her feet and quite indignant. However, whatever the young man said pacified her, and after speaking briefly to her husband, she left the room to change her clothes.

Then the young man approached us. He noticed our wet tablecloth and the overflowing glasses, and his mouth compressed with irritation.

"I am sorry, Mrs. Dunbar. Would you and your niece like another table?"

"We'd like to stay here, sir. But how do you know my name?"

He managed a smile. "I'm Matthew Arneil. I saw my father bring you to this table and noticed the long wait you had for service. I ordered the waiter to your table. Apparently he resented my doing so. He will be dismissed."

"Oh, please don't," my aunt said. "He's probably a bit harried. The dining room is quite full."

"That has nothing to do with it. He behaved poorly."

"Did you see his actions?" I couldn't help but ask the question.

"I saw him fill your glasses and overheard his rudeness. We do not tolerate that. My father told me who you were, by the way."

"Are you working here, Mr. Arneil?" my aunt asked.

"No."

My aunt smiled. "You should be in the diplomatic service. You have pacified everybody."

He returned the smile. "That's part of it. I'm really an architect, and I designed the new hotel. I'm sorry our plans displeased you."

She dismissed it with an airy wave of her hand. "I've gotten over it. As I told your parents, my worst fault has always been my stubbornness, which I must outgrow."

"I'll send a waitress to change your cloth. I hired several from New York. They're very good, and it gives them the opportunity to get away from the sweltering city."

Matthew excused himself. He was gone only moments when a waitress came to take our order. Her eagerness to please more than made up for the surliness of the waiter. Nonetheless, knowing he was going to be dismissed bothered me. It had a depressing effect on my aunt, also, and we remained quiet throughout the meal, other than to comment on the delicious omelette.

Matthew met us in the lobby. He once again apologized for the waiter's rudeness. My aunt told him not to worry, and inquired about the waiter's injuries.

House of Silence

"He has already regained consciousness," Matthew said. "A doctor is attending him. Don't worry. Thank you both for being so understanding. I hope we will meet again soon, Miss Parris."

I felt foolish as I blushed. His statement was meant only as a friendly gesture, I was sure, even though he gazed intently at me. He was easily six feet tall, with dark hair parted in the center, and a lean face. His eyes were a soft gray, and though there had been no occasion for him to smile, I imagined that when he did, it would be warm and friendly.

Outside, we walked over to where Pierce was waiting by our carriage.

My aunt said, "I hope you lunched."

"I did, ma'am," he replied. "They have a separate room for drivers. Delicious food and no charge."

On our way home, I was not thinking of the luxury of the carriage, the beauty of the countryside, or the young and gracious Mr. Arneil.

"What is it, my dear?" my aunt said. "I know you're not silent because of the scenery."

"I'm thinking of that waiter and the fall he took."

"What about it?" my aunt asked.

"I don't understand my own feelings. I really wanted him to make a fool of himself, and I suggested as much."

"You didn't cause him to fall," my aunt said.

"I put the thought in his mind."

"His behavior was obnoxious."

"So were my thoughts," I replied miserably.

"Hold your head up, child. You did nothing shameful. He was so filled with anger that he wasn't paying attention."

"Even so, he not only injured himself, but lost his job."

"He should have," my aunt said. "And so should you or I if we behaved as he did."

"Nonetheless, I feel guilty. I have an uneasy feeling something is happening inside me."

"Whatever are you talking about?" I could sense my behavior was upsetting my aunt, and I didn't want to bring on another one of her headaches, yet I had to say what was on my mind.

"I could go back to the moment of Mama's accident, though I am not really to blame for that. If only I had run to her side and rescued her in time. It was just that she moved so fast, as if a strong force was driving her. A terrifying thought."

"I agree," my aunt said. "And one you must not dwell upon."

I raised my head and looked off into the distance without seeing anything. "I believe it started at the depot yesterday."

"You mean the incident with the little dog?"

"Yes. I spoke words without being aware of it."

"What nonsense," my aunt said softly.

"No more so than what happened in the dining room today. Seriously, Auntie, I believe I knew what was going to happen beforehand."

"My dear child," my aunt protested, "you got up to go to his aid."

"It could have been only pretense. In fact, I know it was."

My aunt rested a comforting hand on my shoulder. "Nila, you have been through a very shattering experience. You won't get over what you saw happen to your mother for quite some time. The shock of what you've endured may be far greater than you can imagine, especially since you have just entered womanhood and always led such a sheltered life at a girls' school. I don't mean this in a critical sense, but you led an abnormal life, after your papa died."

"Drowned," I corrected her.

"Yes," she replied.

House of Silence

"It seems as if tragedy, of one kind or another, is going to be a part of my life."

"You saved that puppy's life," she reminded me.

"And he either hated or feared me. Perhaps the waiter felt the same way."

"Have you forgotten that it was his rudeness to me that caused you to speak up?"

"Nonetheless, I have never spoken like that before. I never behaved in such a fashion in my life."

My aunt patted my arm. "As I told you, you've been through a lot these past few days. Ordinarily, you wouldn't dwell on such minor incidents."

"Forgive me, Auntie. I mustn't upset you. You've been through a lot, too, and I don't want you to get another headache."

"I don't want one either, my dear. I do wish I could help you get rid of your guilt feelings. Since I can't, I may as well make a confession. I know the waiter and his mother. I hold the mortgage on their house. They are always in arrears, and I have not foreclosed on her because she is widowed. I was even going to . . . oh well." She shrugged. "Now that he has been so rude to us, I may give my attorney instructions to foreclose on the property."

"Oh, please don't, Auntie," I pleaded. "That would make me feel worse."

"Very well," my aunt acquiesced. "I had other plans, so I shan't do anything immediately."

"Thank you." I flashed her a grateful smile.

"Just bear in mind that his hatred was directed at me. Oh—I didn't tell you that Peter Rogerson will be at the house when we return. Sometimes he stays with me and sometimes at the inn. That is, of course, when it is open, which has been only in the summer up until now, though I understand Pearl and Andrew are seriously considering keeping it open year-round."

"This area must be growing," I said.

"There are mountains close by where more and

more people come to stay for holiday. And more would come throughout the year if there were facilities. That is one of the things Peter has come to discuss with me. I have extensive property holdings in this area, which I am going to put on the market."

"I should think Mr. and Mrs. Arneil might be interested," I said.

My aunt laughed. "I tried to get them interested before, but they wanted that property across the lake. If they should want to purchase additional property now, they will pay double."

"I thought you were friends, Auntie," I said.

"I never allow friendship to interfere with business, nor would they, I am sure."

"I disagree," I said. "I remember their graciousness. Our luncheon was free today. Their son was most apologetic about what happened and did everything he could to compensate."

My aunt laughed and shook her head. "A clean tablecloth. I don't think that was much of an expense, do you?"

"I'm thinking of the lady's satin gown, which was probably ruined by the water, and the six people at the other table whose lunch ended up on the floor."

"Let us forget the luncheon, my dear. I want to tell you about Peter Rogerson. He's a splendid young man, a member of a famous law firm in Boston, and already he's made a name for himself."

"I shouldn't think you would want to risk having the newest member of the firm representing you."

"I happened to be in the Boston office the first day he was there. Naturally, he was a little nervous, but he was also eager and answered my questions intelligently. I decided that I wanted him to take care of all my transactions. That was two years ago. Besides his business acumen, he has a lot of charm. I know you will like him and will enjoy having someone your age to converse with."

"If he is that intelligent, he will probably be bored by me."

"No, my dear. Even though you are a young woman now, you still have an appealing girlish naivete. Even the young Mr. Arneil was impressed."

"I doubt he noticed me."

She laughed. "Don't play games with your auntie. I saw you blush when he expressed the hope you would meet again."

"He said that to both of us, Auntie," I contradicted.

"He meant you, dear. I predict great things for you."

"In what way?" I asked in amazement.

"Only time will tell. Well, here we are."

Pierce turned into the driveway and started the climb to the house. Halfway up, we saw a horse and buggy.

"Peter is here," my aunt exclaimed with pleasure. "Good. Take care of his animal, Pierce."

"Yes, ma'am."

Pierce helped us down, and we went inside.

"Evelyn, how good to see you." It was Peter Rogerson, calling out as he decended the stairway.

"Peter, you dear boy." My aunt threw her arms around him. He kissed her cheek lightly and turned to me. He wasn't as tall as Matthew, but he was the handsomest young man I had ever seen. Mr. Rogerson had dark brown eyes, strong features, and wavy brown hair. He was wearing white trousers, a white shirt open at the neck, sneakers, and was holding a tennis racket, which he tossed on a chair when he turned to me.

"You are Miss Parris," he said. "Your aunt sent me a telegram, informing me of the tragedy and of her hope that you would return to stay with her. I'm glad you did. I'm sorry about your mother."

"Thank you, Mr. Rogerson. I will never forget my aunt's kindness. I am fortunate she was in New York

City when Mama died. She relieved me of all responsibility."

"That is her way," he said. "I was going to play a game of tennis with Giles, but I'd rather get acquainted with you."

"Please don't disappoint Mr. Lazarno," I said. "Besides, I would like to freshen up."

My aunt said, "It would do us both good to rest a little. You and Peter may get acquainted this evening."

He lifted then dropped his hands at his sides in a gesture of defeat. "I'm afraid we'll have to obey her."

His good nature was infectious and I laughed. "I think her suggestion is sensible."

"With both of you against me, I shall have to be patient."

My aunt dismissed him with a wave of her hand. "Come, Nila. One thing about that luncheon—it wasn't dull."

"Want to tell me about it?" Peter lingered, despite the fact that we had started our ascent up the stairs.

"No," my aunt said in mock sternness. "You'll hear about it later—if Nila wishes to tell you."

"I hope Nila will," Peter called up to us. "Most luncheons I've attended are frightfully dull."

We had reached the top of the stairs, and I looked down at that dark-haired god, who seemed bursting with masculine energy. The thought occurred to me that he needed a good fast game of tennis to calm him down. He was still smiling at me when I turned my head away. I felt his eyes regarded me a little too warmly. If my aunt noticed, she said nothing.

She sighed wearily, and I turned to her. "I hope you aren't getting another headache."

She reassured me with a mild shake of her head. "Just getting old, my dear. The stairs are becoming a trial."

"Francine told me you have trouble with your blood pressure."

House of Silence

"Francine worries about me like a mother hen," my aunt scoffed. "But I couldn't get along without her."

For the first time I remembered the incident on the dark lawn last night. I wondered if she was as loyal to my aunt as she seemed.

Once in my suite, I removed my hat and gloves and started into the bedroom before I heard a sound in the next room. It was Francine. Several long boxes were on the floor. They were the type used by high-class salons for women's garments.

"Your clothes came, mademoiselle," Francine said excitedly. "Everything. Your aunt said to them that she expected fast service. Everything will fit because I remember shortening the black skirt you are now wearing, and I know the measurements."

"How many boxes are there?" I asked in dismay. There was scarcely room to walk.

"I already took some out," she informed me, laughing. "I opened lingerie boxes first, then shoes and slippers. Last—dresses, dinner gowns, afternoon gowns, and much more. The closets and drawers are full."

"Why did my aunt purchase so much?" I asked. "I will never wear it all."

"You will, mademoiselle," she exclaimed. "Your aunt will see to it. She wants you to be happy. You are very brave. You had much sadness when your mama . . ." Her voice broke off, and I thought she was on the verge of tears.

"Thank you, Francine. It is good of you to think that way of Mama when you never knew her."

"Your aunt has pictures of her and your papa. I know she was a lovely lady. And your papa—handsome. But Frenchmen are. They have a way." She gave a delicate shrug.

"Are you happy, Francine?" I asked.

My question startled her. "*Mais oui*. Why do you ask?"

"I really don't know why I asked," I said. "I sup-

51

pose because there is no one around here for you, other than Mr. Lazarno, and he is much too old."

"He is very handsome, don't you think?" Her face lit up at the sound of his name.

"Very handsome. So is Mr. Rogerson. Is every gentleman who comes here that handsome?"

"You would call Pierce Lavery handsome?" She made it a question.

"Hardly." Our voices mingled in laughter.

She once again became serious. "I'll gather up these boxes and let you have a rest. Did you enjoy luncheon, mademoiselle?"

I sobered at the thought of it. "The food was delicious, but I am tired. I'd like to take a nap."

"I'll be quick, mademoiselle."

As I assisted her with the boxes, I asked, "Which wing do you sleep in, Francine?"

"I have a room next to your aunt's suite. Why do you ask? Are you afraid in this wing by yourself?"

"Oh, no."

"No need to be. Mr. Giles and Mr. Peter are in the far wing. That is a long way from here."

"I wasn't even thinking of them," I said.

"No, mademoiselle," she said politely. "I'll leave you now. Sleep well, *s'il vous plait*."

I noticed I had a headache. The incident with the waiter at the hotel had upset me more than I realized. I lowered the shades and lay down. Just as I was dismayed by what had happened to the waiter, I was touched by Mr. Arneil's concern for us. I remembered him expressing the hope he would see us again, and my aunt saying he was referring to me. I pressed the cool sheet against my face as I felt a warm flush envelop my body at the thought of him.

Gradually, the darkness of the room and the coolness of the sheets relaxed me, and I drifted off to sleep.

FOUR

"Mademoiselle, please wake up. You will be late for dinner."

I sighed as I opened my eyes. I had fallen into a deep sleep and found it difficult to wake up. But Francine kept calling to me, and I finally focused my eyes on her.

"That is the first restful sleep I have had since Mama died," I said sleepily.

"I am glad, *cherie,* but you must get up. You cannot tarry. Only one-half hour you have. Your aunt demands promptness."

Reluctantly, I pushed my feet off the bed and sat there until I was fully awake.

Francine held up a gown. "Look, mademoiselle. This is the beautiful gown I have selected for you to wear tonight."

"It is beautiful," I agreed, "but I think I should wear black."

"No, *cherie.*" She spoke with quiet firmness. "This is modest. Long sleeves, high neck. Look at how full the back and sides of the skirt are. And look how pretty. You will look like a doll."

"Hardly that," I said, laughing. "But I will wear it."

"You will please your aunt. She will know you like her gifts."

"Oh, I like them, Francine," I said. "It's just that it seems more like a gown one would wear to a happy gathering."

"Make the dinner a happy gathering," Francine pleaded. "You do not know how much your aunt wants you to be happy."

"I'm beginning to. You needn't stay, Francine. I can manage."

"Yes. You learned to be chic at that school."

I thanked her and put on fresh undergarments. I wasted no time, having sensed Francine's nervousness at finding me still asleep.

I styled my hair with short tendrils across the brow and drew the rest back. The dress was a modest gown, yet beautiful—and daring—with its long shirred sleeves of sheer lace.

Mr. Rogerson awaited me at the head of the stairs and offered his arm. He looked elegant in evening clothes.

"You look charming, Nila," he said. "Your aunt has instructed both Giles and me to address you by your given name, and you are to do the same with us."

"She should have consulted me first," I said quietly. "I am not used to addressing gentlemen by their first names on so short an acquaintance."

"I sense that you have known very few gentlemen."

"You are right."

"Then we shall refrain from calling you Nila until you give your permission," he said courteously.

I shrugged. "If my aunt wishes it, you may do so."

"Only if you will use my given name. Please."

I hesitated a second then gave a brief nod.

His smile was winning. "Thank you, Nila. I must compliment you on your gorgeous gown."

"My aunt has spent a fortune on me."

"Be assured she has it to spend," he replied.

"I just wish she wouldn't. I'm not used to such luxuries."

"Don't you like them?"

"Yes," I admitted. "But I don't need them. Mama and I were happy with very little."

House of Silence

"I understand, but try to think of your aunt's years of loneliness. She is a recluse."

"So I see. Yet, despite her generosity, I doubt I could live here forever."

He looked amused. "I'm sure she wouldn't expect you to be her constant companion. You must become acquainted with adults closer to your age."

"Yes," I agreed. "However, that doesn't mean I'm not grateful to her."

"I am sure she considers these luxuries your due," Peter replied.

"I don't." I didn't wish to pursue the subject further and said, "My aunt told me you're a brilliant lawyer."

"I've been lucky. From the day I started practice, I entered a new world, one I hadn't been aware existed."

"Are you referring to the business world?"

"More than that. We'll talk of it later."

Giles and my aunt were already waiting for us in the dining room. He seated my aunt at the head of the table, and Peter seated me at her right.

Pierce served roast chicken, sage stuffing, mashed potatoes, and fresh corn for the main course. Afterwards, we remained at the table drinking our coffee. Giles and Peter kept the conversation light. I mostly listened, but I did mention the incident at the inn.

"Do you have the power to predict?" Peter asked.

"Good gracious, no," I exclaimed. "At least I hope not."

"That is a gift, my dear," Giles said. "One couldn't dismiss what happened at the depot and again today as coincidence."

"What happened at the depot?" Peter asked.

"I don't want to talk about it," I said.

"It's nothing to be ashamed of, Nila," my aunt said. "By the way, you look charming in your new gown."

"Forgive me for not yet thanking you, Auntie."

"You are a great comfort to me," she said quietly. "And although what happened at the inn distressed you, I am aware that you spoke up only because of the waiter's behavior toward me."

"Please," Peter pleaded, "will someone tell me what happened at the depot?"

My aunt said, "Nila saved the life of a little puppy."

"That's something you can take pride in," Peter said.

"I don't, considering the little dog's reaction toward me."

My aunt said, "Peter will pester you until he knows the story, so I will tell him just what happened."

When she finished, he addressed me. "I don't blame you for being hurt, but it would be foolish to dwell on it. I would say you do have a gift of some sort."

"You're talking nonsense," I said.

"Nila refuses to take any credit." My aunt patted my hand reassuringly. "I suggest that Peter take you on a tour of those rooms which comprise our private museum. Or so Giles calls it."

"What else could you call it?" Giles asked.

"I'd be delighted." Peter was already on his feet.

"Wouldn't you rather have a glass of brandy with Giles?" I was surprised at the ease with which his name slipped off my tongue.

"No." Peter reached for my hand. "I feel I'm in the company of someone exceptionally talented. Come, Nila, let me show you your aunt's priceless collections."

"What do you mean by talented?" I asked. His hand still held mine as we moved in the direction of the museum.

The walls of the first room were covered with paintings. Though the room wasn't very large, three chandeliers hung from the ceiling.

Peter released my hand and picked up a pair of lamps. He led the way, pointing out the most outstanding oils by the old masters.

"Your uncle was quite a collector," he said.

"I can see that." It was impossible to observe each

painting in one visit. I studied only the most interesting oils.

"Some of these," he said in an undertone, "were stolen from museums in this country and in Europe."

"How do you know?" I was flabbergasted.

"I'm a bit of an art connoisseur. Of course, although I knew, I never mentioned it to your aunt. However, she told me once that she'd known all along."

"Did she approve of it?" I asked in astonishment.

"No, but her husband said he wanted them and didn't care how he got them."

"I'm glad I never knew him," I said. "Great art should be enjoyed by the public. Selfishness is bad enough, but to acquire something this valuable through chicanery, is sickening."

"Your aunt and I agree," Peter said. "But she had no say in the matter."

"Surely she could have given them back to the museums after her husband's death."

"Yes," Peter agreed. "She discussed it with me, but she couldn't bear the shame and embarrassment. However, according to her will, when she dies they will be sent back to the proper places. I shouldn't have told you, because I don't want you to think ill of her."

"I'm glad I know."

"Come. I'll show you a room filled with legitimately acquired Chinese art treasures."

We entered another room containing screens of hammered silver and jade statues of every size and description. There were also chess and backgammon sets of jade and ivory. Each item had a small, typewritten card describing it's origin.

"It's unbelievable," I said, moving from table to table. "It seems such a waste not to have these pieces available to the public. You know, this house should be turned into a museum."

"You're right," Peter agreed. "That's what it is."

"I wonder if the thought ever occurred to my aunt," I mused. "She doesn't need this big house."

"I would move cautiously," Peter said quietly. "This is her home, and she is quite proud of it. Until you came here, it was all she had. Have you walked around the grounds yet?"

"There hasn't been time," I said.

"When you do, you will understand what I mean. A fortune has been spent on them. Gardeners are brought in from Boston once a week."

"A museum can have beautiful grounds, also," I said.

"Are you suggesting that I plant such an idea in your aunt's head?" Peter asked, a half smile on his face.

"I may do it myself," I said seriously.

"If you do," he said, "I'll back you up. I believe you would be more successful than I."

"Let us move on to the next room," I said.

"I'm glad you didn't find this one depressing," he said. "The next one is somewhat similar. Instead of paintings, it has statuary and beautiful marble pillars engraved from top to bottom with Roman history."

I was astonished and fully aware of how difficult they must have been to come by. "Were they acquired honestly?" I asked.

"No," he admitted. "There is also a Greek room and a Roman room. Most of the art was smuggled into the country."

"I don't wish to see either. Is there anything else?"

"Yes." He set the lamp down and opened the door.

"Are the chandeliers in these rooms lit all the time?"

"Oh, no. Only when their contents are shown."

"I wonder how many have seen them."

"Very few, I imagine."

"Perhaps I am the first, besides those close to my aunt."

"Perhaps," he admitted with a smile. "The room in

House of Silence

which everything has been obtained legally is the third door down. I wouldn't say it contains valuables. The artifacts are of dubious worth, which you may find interesting."

"I am curious."

This third room was lit by candlelight. After the other rooms I had been in, this shadowy one was eerie. There were drawings on the walls and an exquisite petit point tapestry. Directly opposite the door was an altar. On the painted black floor was a white double circle with strange writing, and four stars pointing north, south, east, and west.

"What is this?" I asked, thoroughly puzzled.

"Have you ever heard of witchcraft?" Peter asked.

"We had a course at school about the Salem witch hunt. But we never believed those poor women were guilty of casting spells."

"People in this state still take it seriously," he said.

"Surely you don't," I said. I walked to the altar and looked down at the various items laid out in order on a black embroidered cloth. There were two knives, a chalice, a sword, a cord, a piece of metal resembling a serpent, a large, rather shallow, heavily embossed sterling silver dish, a wand, a cat-o'-nine-tails. There was also a metal artifact, where incense was burned.

Peter said, "Each object on that altar has a part in the initiation rites."

"The cat-o'-nine-tails has no place on an altar."

"It does on this one, but the initiate is whipped very lightly."

"What is the silver dish for?" I asked, more to make conversation than from interest.

"Oil is poured in it at the beginning of the ceremony. Certain parts of the initiate's body are anointed."

I turned to face him. "You know all about it, don't you?"

He smiled. "I grew up hearing about witchcraft. My grandmothers swore they were witches."

"It must have been frightening for you."

"At first, yes. But little by little I acquired more than a casual interest in it. By the time I was grown, I knew I was a warlock."

"A male witch."

He smiled. "You do remember your lessons."

I looked at the closed door. Above it, spelled out in gold, was the word *wicca*. I spoke the word, then asked its meaning.

"*Wicca* means witchcraft," Peter said. "Everything pertaining to witchcraft is in this room. A coven of witches could meet here and perform their rites without the slightest inconvenience."

"I recall that coven means a group of witches."

Peter raised his arms and swept them outward to encompass the entire room. "This could be a covenstead—the meeting place of a coven."

"Surely my aunt would not countenance such a thing."

He laughed. "I've never asked her."

"I feel repelled by it," I said, eyeing the drawings on the wall with distaste.

"This is the first time you have been in here. Mark my words, you will be drawn back. Do you know why?"

"I think the wine we drank at dinner has let your imagination run wild."

"Not true. You will be drawn back here, just as I am. You have the gift of foretelling."

"Are you referring to the dog and the waiter?"

"Yes."

"Nonsense," I exclaimed indignantly. "Even if I did, I'm not a witch."

"Perhaps not. But don't upset yourself. Do you wish to examine anything here?"

"I would like to run out of here, but I won't. I shall examine the room a little more closely so that I can prove to you I don't fear it and that I could never be a part of such evil."

"Witches do good," he said seriously, "though they can also do evil."

"Surely you're not branding me a witch because of what happened to the poor waiter."

"I'm not branding you anything. It might be you cannot help yourself."

I shifted my glance to him and spoke with a stern and disapproving tone. "I am not a witch. Nor do I believe that you are a warlock."

"But I am," he said laughing. "I practice witchcraft in my profession with marvelous luck."

"I suggest you not let my aunt hear you speak in such a fashion. She thinks highly of you."

"I'm aware of that. Please don't be angry with me, Nila. Come to the altar. I want to show you something."

I did so unenthusiastically. He picked up the crystal ball. "Look into it and tell me what you see. It can't hurt you."

I held it. "Nothing but clear crystal."

"Stop being annoyed with me and keep looking."

Slowly, the face of a strange woman appeared in the glass. She was very thin, with sunken eyes, colorless lips, and her clothes hung on her emaciated frame.

"I do see someone," I exclaimed in alarm. "But I don't know who she is."

He took the glass from me. "Don't let it frighten you. You see, you have the gift. You must learn to use it wisely."

I was trembling inside and shaken by the woman's face. My attention was drawn to a book on the altar, entitled *Book Of Shadows*.

"That is the book of rules for a witch or warlock," Peter explained. "You can also read them in the beautiful stitchery on the tapestry hanging on that wall."

I walked over and studied the petit point. Despite

the dim light, the work was so exquisite that the words were quite clear.

It began:

The Law

1. The Law was made and ordained of old.
2. The Law was made for followers of *wicca,* to advise and help in their troubles.

I impatiently shook my head. "It's all too ridiculous."

I switched my attention to the drawings on the wall and gasped aloud.

"What is it?" Peter was by my side.

"Nothing. The figures startled me for a moment."

"That's a drawing of a coven."

I nodded, but couldn't reply. They were wearing robes exactly like the one Francine had been wearing the night I saw her wandering on the grounds.

"Is that what they wear?" I asked.

"That is the official garment."

I said, "This room disgusts me."

"I hope I don't."

"I'm so confused and mixed up I don't know what I think of you. Forgive me, Peter, but I must be honest. That was practically a creed between Mama and me."

"You were very close to her, weren't you?"

"We had only each other."

"That is what you thought. Aren't you glad your aunt found you?"

"Yes," I admitted. "It frightens me to think of being alone. I had no idea Mama earned so little. She certainly managed well."

"You may not know it, but that was also your aunt's doing."

"My aunt was truly penitent, wasn't she?"

"You could say that. Or it might be she was thinking of you, concerned about you, and keeping track of both you and your mother."

"That wasn't difficult. Mama never left the academy."

"Your aunt saw to that," Peter said. "And wasn't it better to have those surroundings than a cold-water walkup?"

I nodded. "Please, let's leave this room."

He took my hand again, but when he slowed to close the door behind us, I slipped free. Somehow, Peter didn't seem like the same person I had met earlier. I repressed a shudder as the thought occurred to me that I wasn't the same either. I was becoming unsure of myself, wondering if I had made a wise move in coming up here. Yet where else could I have gone? It was the face of that emaciated woman in the crystal that had unnerved me. I wondered who she was.

Peter led me to the large parlor where Giles and my aunt were enjoying their drinks. Giles stood up when we entered and asked if I would like a glass of wine. I refused, but Peter accepted brandy, cupping his hands around the base of the snifter to warm it.

I sat beside my aunt."

"Did you enjoy the museum, dear?" she asked with a smile.

"All except the last room," I replied. "That frightened me."

"It does frighten those who see it for the first time. Often, though, people ask if they might see it a second and third time."

"Do you grant permission?"

"Only if they are sincere."

"Surely you don't believe in witchcraft, Auntie."

"I keep an open mind regarding *wicca*," she said.

"And you Giles?" I asked.

He smiled down at me. "I find it bewitching, my dear. But then, I find you bewitching, also."

"I don't want to be like a witch. I suppose those symbols on the altar are a part of their rituals."

"Everything in that room pertains to witchcraft," Giles said.

"I saw a strange woman's face in the crystal. She is very ill."

My aunt was so startled she dropped her glass of sherry. Giles offered his handkerchief.

I said, "I'm sorry I spoiled your gown. I didn't mean to frighten you."

"You startled me," she said. "What did the woman look like?"

I described her, and my aunt regarded me with amazement. "That is Mrs. Mercy Ambrus, the mother of the waiter."

It was my turn to be surprised. My aunt went on. "Peter has never met her, but he will tomorrow."

"Auntie," I exclaimed, "please don't foreclose on her."

She chuckled. "Relax, Nila. I knew how upset you were about what happened, and I decided that perhaps you would forget the incident more quickly if I forgave the mortgage. Peter is bringing it to her tomorrow."

"Please let me go with you, Peter," I exclaimed. "I want to meet Mrs. Ambrus and inquire about her son. I hope his injuries weren't serious."

"I doubt they were," my aunt replied. "In fact, I'm certain they were not. Don't worry about him."

"How could you know, Auntie?" I asked.

"We would have heard something," she said.

"He'll be just fine," Peter said. "It was in the crystal."

"I didn't see his features," I said.

"I did—when I took the ball from you."

"I have a little business to attend to with Peter and Giles," my aunt said. "Will you excuse us, dear? You may go to the music room if you wish."

"I would rather go upstairs and look at my new wardrobe," I said.

"I hope you like it."

"Don't ever doubt it." I bent and kissed her cheek. "May I go with Peter tomorrow?"

"I won't be coming back," he said. "Pierce was going to drive me to the village and then the depot."

"You have a buggy, don't you, Auntie?" I asked. "Pierce could return with me."

"Yes, but . . . I wouldn't want any harm to come to you."

"Don't worry," I said. "When do we leave?"

"At nine," Peter said. "I must catch the train to Boston."

My aunt addressed him. "I'll expect you back soon."

"I shan't tarry," he promised.

She said, "All right, my dear. You may go with him, though I'll worry until you return."

I laughed at her concern, though it showed she cared. "I'll return safe and sound, Auntie. Good night."

I excused myself and went to my room. My mood changed once I was in bed, and my thoughts kept returning to the covenstead. I would not allow myself to believe it had ever been used by witches. The longer my mind dwelled on it, the more restless I became.

I decided to inspect my new wardrobe—anything to shut out visions of *wicca*. There was every type of apparel, from a tennis outfit to a formal gown. I should have been ecstatic at my good fortune, but visions of the covenstead continued to haunt me.

I put the clothing back in the closet, and sat down. My mind was too preoccupied with what was in that room to sleep. I knew that what troubled me was far more frightening than what I was about to do.

I put out the lamps and moved cautiously from my suite. I had reached the end of the corridor when I heard the front door open and then close again quietly. The sound of whispering voices reached my ears. It seemed to be some sort of argument, though I could not make out what was being said. When a few words drifted up to me, I knew why. They were speaking in French. I knew the language, but their muted tones kept me from hearing the conversation.

A trace of flickering light flashed now and then, and I realized they were climbing the stairs. I heard a sound, and then the light steadied.

I was frozen in fear of discovery. The voices continued. I pressed my body against the wall. I needed only to take a step in order to be in full view of whoever was standing at the head of the stairs.

"It is humiliating for me to have her come here for initiation."

"Where else would she be initiated?"

I wondered if they were discussing me, and what sort of initiation they were talking about.

"When is she coming?" That question eliminated me.

"In a few days. With Peter."

"Why can't he . . . ?"

They were speaking softly now. I realized it was Francine who had asked the last two questions.

"I am the high priest." Giles was supplying the answers. "We must obey the high priestess."

"What if she learns about us?" Francine asked.

"We'll end up without a roof over our heads. Remember the vow of obedience you took?"

"Peter could please her," Francine insisted. "Let him initiate her."

"No doubt. But she is not a fool, and she is too old for Peter. Don't forget, I follow instructions also."

"Does she think you love her?" Francine asked scathingly.

"Possibly. She is starved for affection. She will serve us well. We need her."

"I don't need her," Francine said. "I need you. I can't bear to think of your arms around her, making love to her as you go through the ceremony."

"You know I've initiated others," he said softly. "Some were older than she. We need young ones to carry on our work, and she can be the means of our getting them. Those we get from the inn are almost as old as Evelyn."

"I could kill her." Francine was still overwrought. "Do you make love to her?"

"No."

"But once . . ."

"That was long ago. Before she discovered you in Paris. We need her. We like this life."

"What about the niece?"

"What about her?"

"Will she come to us?"

"Of course she will. She has the power. I told you what she saw in the crystal tonight. With realization will come courage."

"I don't know. She has the gift, but . . ."

"Now, my pet, we have finished our work for the night. Kiss me and stop asking questions."

"I should not," Francine said fretfully. "You should want only me."

"I do, my pet," was the soothing reply.

When Nila is initiated, will . . . ?"

"Peter will initiate her. I have a feeling Evelyn has great plans for them. Now kiss me and stop talking."

The silence which followed meant Francine had given in. I risked a glance around the corner to see them.

They were locked in an embrace, and both were wearing the hooded cloaks. I drew back quickly, without being seen. The light from the candle extended only halfway down the corridor, but it was bright enough to reveal their bare feet.

A weakness brought on by fear encompassed me. I felt as if I had guilelessly walked into a web of intrigue and evil that had been spun for me. Was my aunt a witch? Could she cast spells? Could Giles? Could Francine? And Peter? What about me? Certainly I had seen Mrs. Ambrus in the crystal ball. I now knew some power greater than mine had caused me to save the puppy's life. I felt completely responsible for all that had happened to George Ambrus.

"Come to my suite," Giles said softly, his voice charged with emotion.

"She might awaken and call for me." Francine's voice held a touch of fear.

"She won't. I saw to it that the sleeping potion you gave her was extra strong. Of course, if you are too tired, or if my company bores you . . ."

"You are so egotistical. I should say good night and go to my room," Francine scolded.

"But you won't, my pet."

"No," she admitted. "Fool that I am. But I hate that woman."

"Which one?"

"Both. They are old fools."

"Forget them or I'll send you to your room—and lower your voice. Just because your mistress took a sleeping potion doesn't mean Peter did."

"Sometimes I think he is jealous because you are high priest of our coven."

"Perhaps. But he'll not risk my casting a spell on him."

"What if he casts one on you?"

"He won't. His interest is in Nila, who will inherit everything. We must be careful to treat him with the utmost respect. He is making contacts in Boston which will gain us converts."

"Let them be male converts. So that Miss . . ."

Their voices were fading, and I didn't hear the name she spoke.

However, the mention of it irritated Giles, for he forgot his caution and raised his voice sufficiently for me to hear, "I told you to forget her."

The door closed, and the hall was silent. I peeked around the corner and saw that they had taken the candle with them. I didn't mind the darkness, for I was

House of Silence

familiar with the house and could find my way to the covenstead. I had been relieved to learn that my aunt had taken a sleeping potion.

I entered the room easily and closed the door. I had seen a box containing matches on the table just inside the door. My hands moved carefully on the tabletop, and I found the box.

I struck a match, and the flame took hold as I touched it to the candles set in a candelabrum. At once an eerie light flooded the room. I went to the altar and studied the tools of witchcraft more carefully. I had no idea of their meaning or use. I supposed only witches knew.

I took my time walking around the altar. I wondered if everybody in this house was a member of a coven. I wasn't certain if my aunt was a witch, and I wondered about Pierce and Dulcy. I wondered if the couple would stay if they knew about this room and that they lived with witches and warlocks.

I noticed an incense burner on the altar. Behind it, a thick book similar to a bible lay open on a low table. I lit a nearby candle and bent over the book. There were several names in it, none of which were familiar to me. I wondered if it was a genealogy. I turned to previous pages and found my aunt's name. Francine's, Giles's, and Peter's were there also. Two more names leaped off the page at me—those of Dulcy and Pierce Lavery.

Prickles of apprehension broke out over my body. I wondered if I was a prisoner in this house and what type of person my aunt really was. I closed the book and looked at the leather cover. Etched in gold lettering were the words *Witches and Warlocks*.

This book listed the names of all known witches and warlocks. I no longer needed to hear my aunt say she was one. I recalled snatches of conversation which before had puzzled me; I remembered Giles toying with words about being bewitched, and Peter openly avowing he practiced the art—if such it could be called. Peter claimed he had become highly successful through it, and firmly believed he possessed the gift.

Once again I felt like I wanted to escape this room. I blew out the candle that threw light on the cursed book. I stepped into the circle and paused directly in the center. I looked down at the symbols and strange words, and I turned slowly, observing the four stars. I glanced over at the objects on the altar. I was not afraid in this room, yet I had no wish to acquire any knowledge of what part the tools of witchcraft on the altar played in the ceremonies.

I left the room and returned to my suite, more angry than frightened. Once in bed, a thought came to me. Francine and Giles had been outside and were wearing robes. They had mentioned that the covenstead was ready for the initiation of a young woman. I wondered when that would take place—and where the covenstead was. Then I remembered the night I had seen Francine on the estate, on her way to some undisclosed destination. Wherever it was, perhaps the rest of the household had already assembled and was awaiting her arrival. I would make it a point to explore the estate and the surrounding forest. It was possible that a covenstead had been erected in a clearing, where ceremonies could be conducted in secret. I recalled Giles mentioning that he got his exercise chopping wood.

I recalled that I'd wished to go to the village with Peter. I was eager to see the reaction of Mrs. Ambrus when she learned my aunt had forgiven her mortgage. I realized that it still wouldn't help her son, who had lost his job. I wondered if Mr. and Mrs. Arneil would rehire him. It wouldn't hurt to intercede, particularly since I felt I was to blame for everything. My brain became a jumble of thoughts merging into one another, so that nothing made any sense. It was merely nature's way of letting drowsiness overtake me, shutting out my fears so that sleep could give my mind and body a much-needed rest.

FIVE

Once again, Francine awakened me. I had slept deeply and felt quite refreshed.

The ride to the Ambrus home was pleasant. Peter was charming, and we chatted about Boston. I made it a point to keep away from any conversation about witches and warlocks.

The Ambrus residence was on a side street in the village proper. We stopped in front of their clean, white house, which was surrounded by an equally sparkling white fence.

"They keep it up well," I said.

"Your aunt had it painted two weeks ago," he replied. "She knew Mrs. Ambrus was doing poorly, and didn't want her to worry about losing the house. So before she forgave the mortgage, she had it painted for them."

"I'm glad," I said.

"Would you like to tell her the good news?"

"Yes," I said. "But since you are my aunt's attorney, I think she might prefer speaking with you."

"Tell you what—we'll both go to the door."

He gave me an envelope from his portfolio. After helping me down from the buggy, he said, "I'll let you do the honors."

"I wonder how her son is."

"You'll find he's greatly improved."

"I hope so. I wonder how his spirits are after being fired from his job at the inn."

We knocked on the door. It opened almost instantly.

I was too astonished to speak, for it was the same woman I had seen in the crystal. She looked very poor. I felt guilty thinking of my closet filled with clothes.

"What is it, young lady?" Her voice was harsh, and her manner impatient. "Stop staring and say what you're here for."

"I'm sorry, Mrs. Ambrus. My name is Nila Parris. I am Mrs. Dunbar's niece. She asked me to give you this. It's the mortgage on your home, which she has canceled. The place is yours."

She stepped back and regarded me with fear. "Another witch. Another dirty witch. My son told me about you. He said you bewitched him at the inn and made him lose his job. I won't send my thanks to the old witch. And I won't thank you."

"You're a very ungrateful woman," Peter said quietly. "This young lady is not at fault because of what happened to your son."

"Oh, yes, she is, She'll do something to you sooner or later, just as her aunt did to my husband. The roof of this house leaked, and my husband went to her and asked, in a gentlemanly way, if she wouldn't please repair it. She told him he'd have to do it himself, even if it killed him. Those were her words, sir. Her exact words. He had a lung sickness and no strength, and our boy was too young then to help. My husband went up the ladder to the roof and fell off because she cursed him. He died from the fall, as she knew he would."

"If he was that weak, he should not have climbed to the roof. He wouldn't need to be cursed to fall."

"We're not the only ones. She's done it to others in the village."

I still held the envelope containing the mortgage. "Please take it."

"Not from your hand. Drop it. I'll pick it up."

House of Silence

I stared at her unyielding pose for a moment, then gave it to Peter.

He said, "I am Mrs. Dunbar's attorney. Will you take it from me?"

Her hand reached out and snatched the envelope from him, then concealed it beneath her shawl as if she believed he might try to retrieve it.

"Good day, Mrs. Ambrus," Peter said.

She gave him a brief nod, ignoring me completely, and then slammed the door.

The encounter left me shaken. Peter squeezed my arm in a reassuring manner as we returned to the buggy.

"Don't dwell on it. I wasn't aware of her husband's death."

"You don't believe my aunt put a curse on him, do you?"

"If she did, she had a reason."

"You're defending her," I said.

"I don't see it that way."

I didn't pursue the subject. There had been enough unpleasantness. He helped me into the carriage, and then got in himself. "Hold on, Nila. This horse is going to have to move fast to get me to the depot in time. The train is due any minute."

He had no sooner finished speaking than I heard the shrill whistle of the train. It was a breathtakingly short ride. He brought the horse to a stop before the depot, grabbed his portfolio, gave me a hasty kiss on the cheek and an impish smile, and jumped down from the vehicle. He disappeared inside the depot, just as the train started to depart.

I slid over to the driver's seat, but didn't pick up the reins until the train had disappeared. I wanted to be certain Peter had managed to get on it.

I couldn't get George Ambrus or his mother out of my mind. One needed only to look at the bones almost protruding through the old woman's shrunken skin

73

and her sunken eyes to be aware of her poor health. She and her son needed food. He must work in order to provide for the two of them.

I let the horse assume an easy pace after his quick run. His coat glistened with sweat, and he was quite content to laze along. I wanted a little time to think, anyway. What I was about to do was presumptuous, but I had to gamble on the young Mr. Arneil's compassion. Of course, it might be he had nothing to say about rehiring a waiter. Then again, if he had been instrumental in having him dismissed, he might have the authority to rehire him. In any case, I decided I must try.

I drove up to the entrance of the inn, where a man in a livery costume took charge of my horse. I went inside and asked the desk clerk if Mr. Matthew Arneil was about. He suggested I take a seat in the lobby while he checked.

I did so, and in no more than a minute young Arneil entered, his friendly smile much in evidence as he greeted me.

I stood up as I spoke. "Mr. Arneil, is there someplace we can talk in private?"

"I have a suite on this floor. My parents have a nicer one across the way, but they're in a business conference.

I laughed. "It doesn't matter where we talk, just so we won't be overheard."

"Then we'll go to mine."

It was on a corridor off the lobby. The sitting room had large, leather-upholstered chairs and a long divan. There was an architect's drawing board by one window.

"Please sit down, Miss Parris. Have you eaten?"

"Not since breakfast."

"I haven't either, so I'll order two lunches sent in. Please excuse me."

He was gone only a few moments, then returned. "I suggested a salad dish and iced lemonade."

"That sounds delightful. I have just come from the depot. I rode into the village with Mr. Peter Rogerson. Do you know him?"

"We met briefly in Boston. He's done extremely well in his profession."

"I'm sure you've done just as well in yours."

"I'm a few years older than he. In two months, I'll be thirty."

"I suppose you're very busy drawing up plans for the new inn."

"They're already completed. Much as I hate to tell you, the digging will start in two weeks. We'd like the foundation laid before winter, and have hired extra workers from Boston. There isn't enough labor here."

"Where will you house them?"

"We've erected a barracks where they can eat and sleep."

"Then you've had no trouble getting help."

"Indeed not—though we could use more."

"Mr. Arneil, I'm here to ask a favor of you."

"I'll be happy to grant it if it's at all possible. I'd like to think that, if I do, you will allow me to visit you at your aunt's."

"Haven't you ever been there?" I asked.

"No. I understand it's quite a showplace."

"I would say so. I'm quite overwhelmed by it."

"Why should you be? After all, you must have been there many times."

"I didn't know I had an aunt until Mama's accident."

He eyed me strangely, but had no chance to speak before a waiter announced our lunch.

A busboy brought in a table with a collapsible stand. Then a waitress came in, transferred our lunch from the tray to the table, and departed.

They'd served delicious chicken, potato, and vegetable salads. The drive and heat had combined to make me very thirsty, and I was pleased to see an entire pitcher of tangy, cold lemonade.

"I'm surprised that you didn't know your aunt until recently," he said.

"You know about my mother's strange accident. It so happened my aunt was in New York City at the time. She read about it in a newspaper and wrote me a note. Mama was a housemother at a girls' school in the Bronx. My aunt—without Mama's knowledge—had kept track of us. In fact, if it weren't for my aunt, Mama wouldn't have been housemother."

He smiled, but at the same time shook his head. "I'm more puzzled than ever."

"I don't wonder," I said, managing a half smile. "It puzzled me also."

"I assume your aunt and your mother were not friends."

"That is true. My aunt objected to Mama's marriage. Papa had neither money nor social standing. My aunt married a man who had both but I'm sure she was no happier than Mama."

"I never knew of your mother, but the little I know of you is all good."

His statement upset me. I lowered my eyes to conceal the guilt I feared might be revealed.

"Did I say something wrong?" Mr. Arneil asked.

"No. Please let me finish my story. Mama never forgave my aunt for not accepting Papa. My aunt tried to reconcile later, but Mama refused. It was through my aunt's good graces that Mama got the position as housemother after Papa's death. He had taught French there."

"How did your aunt accomplish that?"

"She gave generous endowments to the school, unbeknownst to Mama, who would never have countenanced such a thing."

"Why not?"

"Mama denied my aunt's existence. When she was dying, I told her that her sister Evelyn had asked for her forgiveness. Mama's reply was that she had no sister."

"That's strange, when she knew she was dying."

"I thought so, too. It wasn't like Mama. I'm not so sure now."

"Why?"

"Do you believe in witchcraft?" I'd had no intention of asking the question. It slipped off my tongue as if I couldn't help myself.

His laughter was deep and hearty. "Indeed not."

"It's good to hear you say that, but in a way I almost wish you did."

"I couldn't, Miss Parris. It's a lot of balderdash."

"I thought so too until I arrived here. I have to believe in it now."

"You seem much too sensible and intelligent a young lady."

"Thank you. But it could well be I am a witch. I think my aunt is, and I believe that is the true reason Mama would not recognize her as a sister."

"Please eat your lunch, Miss Parris. You may not realize it, but you are overwrought."

"I am," I admitted. "For one thing, I had an unpleasant experience this morning. Did you know that some of the people in this village also think my aunt is a witch?"

"I've heard gossip to that effect," he said. "Miss Parris, if you don't eat, I will think you don't like our food."

"I do," I declared. "It's just that I am deeply troubled by several things that have happened in the last few days, beginning with Mama's accident."

"Did your mother faint and fall in front of that van?"

"No. We were walking side by side when, without rhyme or reason, she turned suddenly and walked across the sidewalk, deliberately stepping in front of a beer van."

"That is strange," he mused.

"She even commented on it in the hospital during the brief time that she was conscious," I said. "She wondered why she'd done such a stupid thing. I was puzzled by her behavior. She . . ." My voice broke off.

"Do go on," he urged kindly.

"Please forgive me," I said. "I didn't come here to talk about myself. Truly, I didn't."

"Regardless, I would like you to finish this conversation before you tell me why you came—though I am happy you did. I've thought of you a great deal. Now please continue."

She didn't want me to come up here," I said. "She said that Miss Bingham, who owns and runs the academy, wished to hire me as a language tutor."

"But you came here instead," he said.

"I had no choice. Miss Bingham had no desire to hire me after Mama died. I suppose she thought my aunt's endowments would stop."

"You mean your mother's position was contingent on your aunt's generosity to the school?" he asked.

"Miss Bingham admitted it. My aunt had a guilty conscience when it came to Mama. She felt that she had so much and we so little. Yet I know that Mama and I felt that we had a lot."

"By having each other," Mr. Arneil guessed.

"Thank you for understanding. By the way, this is a delicious lunch, and so unexpected."

"I would like you to spend the afternoon here. Is it possible?"

"I wish it were, but my aunt told me she would worry until I returned, so I must get to the point of why I'm here."

"You mentioned something about a favor. If it's in my power, it's already granted."

"It concerns George Ambrus."

House of Silence

Mr. Arneil looked incredulous. "The waiter who was so rude?"

I nodded. "My aunt just canceled Mrs. Ambrus's mortgage."

"Why?" he asked.

"Perhaps because she felt guilty."

"Why should she have?" he asked.

I sighed. "It's difficult to explain."

"Please try."

"Mrs. Ambrus felt no gratitude, either toward my aunt or me. She is bitter because she believes my aunt is responsible for her husband's death."

"How could that be?"

"Mrs. Ambrus believes my aunt and I are witches," I said. "The woman may be right."

He eyed me with concern. "Miss Parris, do you realize what you are saying?"

"Yes. Witches perform good deeds and evil ones. It is called a 'gift,' but I think it's a curse."

He chuckled. "You're a very charming witch."

"I'm not trying to be funny, Mr. Arneil."

"I'm sorry," he said, sobering. "I was hoping to raise your spirits."

"I'm so frightened. I already told you Mama didn't want me to come here. Now I know why, but I had nowhere else to go."

"You did the right thing in accepting your aunt's offer of hospitality. She must be a very lonely woman."

"She claims she is, though I'm not sure she's being honest . . . I shouldn't talk this way when you scarcely know me."

"I don't know your aunt either. My parents have invited her to parties and she has attended from time to time with a gentleman who was a friend of her husband. I understand he has no means of support and lives in her home. My parents believe your aunt is a woman who uses her wealth for good causes and doesn't receive the appreciation she deserves."

"Are you saying she is philanthropic?"

"According to my parents she is. She often pays the doctor bills of poor villagers. When they need surgery, the doctor need only consult her, and they are sent to an excellent hospital in Boston. No one goes hungry in the village, thanks to her."

"Do those who have benefited from her kindnesses express appreciation?"

"I would imagine so," he replied.

"Do you know?"

"Frankly," he said, looking rather sheepish, "I never questioned it."

"How long have you known this?"

His face flushed. "A day or so. I asked my parents about your aunt, only because I wanted to see you again. They said your aunt was a very generous lady."

"Thank you," I murmured, realizing that no matter what I said, I couldn't convince him that either my aunt or I could be witches.

"What was the favor you wished to ask?" he said.

I took a long sip of lemonade before answering. "Forgive me. I forgot how thirsty I was."

"Since you've eaten so little, I'm glad you're drinking." He refilled my glass.

"Will you please rehire George Ambrus? If not here, perhaps you could employ him on your new project."

"Are you serious?" He was openly astonished by my request.

"Completely. His mother is very ill and quite emaciated. What she thinks of my aunt or me is of little consequence. And if my aunt and I can overlook Mrs. Ambrus's hatred of us, can't you?"

He thought a moment, then smiled. "You leave me no choice. I'll go see him. I'm certain my parents would not allow him to work here again, but the construction of our new inn is another matter—it's entirely in my hands. If he will accept that kind of employment, he can be one of the work crew."

House of Silence

"Thank you, Mr. Arneil. Now I can eat my lunch."

"Good. May I pay you a visit sometime soon?"

"If you're not afraid of visiting a witch," I said, managing a laugh.

He eyed me sternly. "I want you to stop talking about witches. I know about the witch trials in the old days, but those ended centuries ago."

"That is what I thought. I shan't say any more about it. You granted my favor, and I shall be ever grateful."

"He will know you were behind this."

"Please, don't mention my name," I said hastily. "Nothing would have happened if it weren't for me."

"Miss Parris, tell me again what your first name is."

"Nila."

"Mine is Matthew. I would like our acquaintance to grow. But you must stop talking such nonsense."

"Or you will think me mad." I smiled at him over the rim of my glass.

"I will think someone is trying to destroy you," he said soberly. "And I'll not allow that to happen."

I was warmed by the firm tone of his voice. No one—other than Mama—had ever spoken to me in such a protective way. "Thank you, Matthew. I shall be very pleased if you can find the time to visit me."

"Be assured I shall waste no time."

"Thank you for the delicious lunch," I said. "And thank you for the favor."

He spoke as he helped me up. "I'm doing it only for you, Nila. Now I would like to ask a favor of you."

"What is it?"

"Forget all this talk of witches. I don't like to see you looking frightened."

"You are a firm disbeliever in witchcraft?"

"I am. Don't let superstitions sway you."

"I shall remember your advice."

He accompanied me to my carriage. After assisting me into my seat, he reached for the reins and handed them to me.

"A safe journey, Nila."

"Thank you, Matthew, for everything."

I caught myself smiling several times during my return journey. The horse was as content as I. Not until I turned into the drive did a depressing feeling engulf me. Regardless of what Matthew said, I had to be a witch, just like my aunt and the other occupants of the house. I wondered if they had scheduled my initiation ceremony. The very thought repelled me, and I wondered how I could escape. I knew Matthew would not help me. How could he, when he placed no credence in what I said? Despite that, he found my company pleasant. As for me, I had never sensed such a feeling of importance. For the first time, I knew the joy of being a woman, admired and respected by a gentleman.

Pierce came out and relieved me of the horse and buggy. Inside, Dulcy told me my aunt wished to see me in her suite.

I had no difficulty finding her rooms. She was seated by a window, and was looking out over the estate. She didn't hear me enter, but turned when I addressed her.

"My dear Nila, I am relieved that you are home. I hope your journey was a pleasant one. You look radiant."

"I have a happy feeling inside me, Auntie," I said.

"Tell me about it." She motioned me to sit down.

"First, of course, we visited Mrs. Ambrus. It wasn't pleasant, but I am warmed by your generosity. She is very ill."

"I was told that by Dr. Woolf. I have asked him to do whatever is possible for her, but he told me there is little he can do. Her entire body is rotting away. He will ease her final days," my aunt said. "Since you returned alone, Peter must have made the train."

"Just barely," I said, smiling.

"I hope you were successful in persuading Matthew Arneil to rehire George Ambrus."

"How did you know I went there?"

House of Silence

"Why shouldn't I know?"

"Because no one knew I was going to do such a thing."

"Let us say I know my niece." She was studying me carefully. "I gather the young Mr. Arneil made quite an impression on you."

"Yes. And he agreed to offer George Ambrus employment at the new inn."

"Oh, dear," my aunt sighed. "If only I weren't so fond of his parents."

"What do you mean?"

She shrugged. "It is of no consequence. Did he tell you his parents invited us to the ball Saturday night?"

"No." I was genuinely surprised.

"Do you wish to go?" she asked. "I was thinking of your mama . . ."

"So was I," I said.

My aunt looked thoughtful. "I believe your mother would wish you to attend. You've led such a sequestered life, and it would do you good to start getting out in the world."

I nodded agreement. "Thanks to you, I have a beautiful gown."

"You are young, my dear," she said. "That is the time when parties are most enjoyable. It will give you an opportunity to meet friends your own age."

"Will you attend?"

"Of course. Giles will escort me. The invitation included a note that Mr. Arneil hoped he might be your escort for the evening. He stated that if he didn't hear from you to the contrary, he would call for you."

"How delightful," I said quietly.

"You're blushing." My aunt laughed softly. "Yes, you are happy inside. I can see the change in you since yesterday. Not even Mrs. Ambrus's bad manners upset you."

"She is so ill—I couldn't resent her behavior."

"I do, but only because it was you on the receiving end. I'm sure she called me a witch."

"And also me."

"And you weren't offended?" My aunt seemed surprised.

"Why should I be when the very idea is preposterous?"

She looked reflective. "I shan't debate that with you just now."

"May I be excused, Auntie? The ride back was tiring."

"Of course, my dear. I am going to nap and I suggest you rest, also."

I went over, kissed her cheek, and went to my suite. I then took a relaxing bath, dressed leisurely, and decided to explore the grounds. In case anyone from the house might be observing me, I thought it would be wise to take a tour of the gardens before I entered the forested area. If anyone was watching and saw me, there would be no reason for them to suspect anything.

SIX

The lawn slanted down to the formal garden. Tall hedges, interspaced with bushes and walks, edged the area. Beyond the first section were the bulb and perennial plants. I walked underneath an arbor, covered with greenery, that ran the length of the garden next to the forest. I was beginning to perspire with the hot sun beating down upon my head, and I welcomed the coolness of the arbor. I soon arrived at a small opening that was barely discernible.

I remembered my reason for exploring, and decided to look for a path. Just as I thought, there was a narrow trail, which I proceeded to follow.

After a while, I began to wonder if it led anywhere. but my efforts were finally rewarded when I emerged into a very wide and circular opening. Set in the midst of it was a round building covered with ivy. I thought at first it might contain gardening tools.

I approached the dwelling and without hesitation opened the door. It was pitch-black inside, and I reached in my pocket for the matches I'd remembered to bring.

I struck one and held it high. It didn't penetrate the gloom, but its light was sufficient to reveal a candle set in a tall brass candlestick. When I lit it, I noticed there were other candlesticks around the edge of the room. I struck another match, lit two more candles, and approached the altar. Yes. it was the covenstead. I felt certain it was the one Francine and Giles had referred to the previous night.

With a number of candles lit, I could now see the entire room. Since I'd entered, I'd not heard a sound, but I now sensed the presence of another person. I believed I even knew who it was.

However, instead of calling on the person to reveal himself, I went to the altar and studied the tools of witchcraft. I lifted the sword and looked at it more carefully. Strange words were engraved on the shaft, and both sides of the blade were razor-sharp.

There was no furniture in the room except for the altar, so the person in there with me had to be crawling on all fours to move around and remain out of my line of vision. The walls and floors were black, except for a white circle before the altar. Inside the double circle were the same unintelligible words and four stars I had seen in the indoor covenstead.

I felt no fear, aware that the hidden individual was the one who was afraid. Still holding the sword, I stepped into the center of the circle and faced the altar. The intruder now had to be crouched behind it.

I said, "Stand up, George Ambrus. I wish to speak to you."

For a moment there was no response. Then there was the sound of movement as first his head emerged, and then his torso as he straightened. His eyes widened in fear at the sight of me, and his mouth was agape. He was too terrified to scream for help.

"What are you doing here?" I asked.

"I came to see if I was wrong. I ain't."

"Wrong about what?" I studied the sword casually as I spoke to him.

" 'Bout you an' your aunt bein' witches. You gonna cast a spell on me?"

"I'm going to try to talk some sense into you. You needn't be afraid of me. Come around the altar."

He made no attempt to move. "You made me act like a fool. I lost my job."

"I didn't mean for that to happen."

"But it did."

"I'm sorry, Mr. Ambrus. I want to make amends."

"You'll put another curse on me," he said fearfully.

"No, I won't. Did you know my aunt canceled the mortgage on your home?"

"With the interest she charged, she should."

"Nonetheless, it now belongs to you and your mother."

"Who's near death from worryin' 'bout bein' put out o' that house."

"She needn't worry anymore. How long have you been here?"

"Since mornin'. I knew there was somethin' evil here. Heard it from one of the villagers who came here to work once. He quit when he saw the goin's on. Didn' live long after. Your aunt put a curse on him."

I wanted to tell him such a thing was preposterous, yet the words wouldn't come. I approached the altar to replace the sword. Apparently he mistook my motives, for he let out a howl of protest and ran around the side of the altar. When I started to walk toward him, he pushed me aside. The sword slipped out of my hand, flew through the air, and imbedded itself in the door, just missing George Ambrus. He cried out again and pulled on the door, forgetting to depress the latch in his terror. He pulled so hard the metal snapped, but the door opened. Fear lent impetus to his retreat, and I heard his running footsteps, coupled with the breaking of branches, as he fled.

I had hoped to make him realize I meant him no harm. Instead, I knew now he would say I had commanded the sword to fly through the air and pierce his body. It did fly through the air, but only because he pushed me with such force it slipped from my hand. Yet it was heavy and should have fallen. I was repelled by the sight of it, still quivering in the door. I didn't want to touch it, but neither did I want anyone to see it.

It took both my hands and all my strength to remove the sword. I threw it on the floor and started to leave the covenstead when I realized the sword should be replaced. I didn't want my aunt to know George Ambrus and I had been in the covenstead. I returned the sword to the altar and moved swiftly to the door, lest George's howls had been heard by someone from the house. I depressed the latch needlessly, as the door could not remain shut by itself now that George had broken the latch. It could be attributed to a vagrant who had gotten on the premises. I found the footpath leading to the arbor and hoped I would not meet anyone on the way. Fortunately, I approached the house completely unseen.

I went to my room and bathed my face in cold water. I was badly shaken from my venture, but not because I had found the covenstead. I had half expected to find some sort of building dedicated to witchcraft in the forest. Nor had George Ambrus's presence upset me. It was only on my way back that I realized I should have been terrified by his presence—yet it had been the other way around. That, added to the shock of the sword flying through the air, disturbed me deeply. I couldn't blame George Ambrus for fearing me. I feared myself. I knew now that I had the cursed gift the others in this house spoke about with pride.

Suddenly I realized that Mama had lived with the fear that I might have inherited the powers of witchcraft. That was why she hadn't wanted me to come here—and why she denied the existence of her sister. Mama had been happy at Miss Bingham's, and she had believed I was safe there. To Mama, witchcraft was evil, and she wished to protect me from it. I didn't want to be a witch, yet the signs pointed to it more and more.

I lay down on the chaise in the sitting room. I wanted to think about a proper course of action to take. I had to get out of here, yet where could I go? I had no money. I couldn't even take Matthew Arneil into my confidence. I wondered what would happen to me if I continued to live here. Would I allow myself to be initiated into the coven?

I drifted off to sleep, still seeking a way to escape. That last thought brought a smile to my lips. I didn't know if I *was* a prisoner, as there was no need for me to be. For the first time I remembered the trunk containing Mama's and my few possessions that Miss Bingham had promised to send. I wondered if it had arrived, or if she had forgotten about it . . .

Francine wakened me. "Please, mademoiselle, it is nine o'clock."

"Oh, dear. Why didn't you waken me earlier?"

She shrugged. "Because your aunt has one of her headaches, and Mr. Giles said he would have dinner in his suite. Would you like yours here?"

"If it isn't too much trouble."

"None," she assured me with a smile.

"A sandwich and some fruit will do."

"Lemonade or coffee?"

"Lemonade, please. I am terribly thirsty."

I was glad I didn't have to dress and go downstairs. I wanted quiet, in order to do more thinking. There had to be a way to resolve my problem—and a way to convince myself I wasn't a witch. The very thought terrified me—as much as my presence in the covenstead had terrified George Ambrus. I realized it was a mixture of fear and bitterness that had caused his rudeness at the inn. I felt no resentment toward his mother for her contempt. She had a good reason to be bitter. I was beginning to sense that my aunt wasn't the person she pretended to be. Her good deads could well be performed to allay any suspicion directed her way. Yet she had not been successful. The villagers accepted her favors because they had no choice—but they would not accept her.

By the time Francine returned, I had donned my nightgown and was seated at the table looking out the window.

She set the tray down, asked if there was anything else I wished, then bade me good night. When I finished eating, I placed the tray on the hall table. There I sat in the darkness, looking out the window for a long time. The rear of the estate was not easy to see because the clouds obscured the moon. I wanted to observe the comings and goings of the occupants of the house, but soon wearied of watching, for there wasn't a sign of anyone.

I heard Francine rearranging the dishes on the tray, and I went to the door.

"Francine, I've been expecting a trunk to arrive from New York City. Has there been any word of it?"

"*Oui*, mademoiselle, it came today. Your aunt gave Pierce instructions to place it in the attic. Do you wish me to tell her you want it brought down to your suite?"

"No, thank you. Just so I know its whereabouts."

"Very well, mademoiselle. Is there anything else you wish?"

"I want to thank you for a delicious supper."

"It was nothing. I understand you are going to the ball with the Arneils' son. He is very charming. Like Peter, only more so."

"You have a charm of your own, Francine," I said, smiling. She did. I could understand why she captivated Giles, and only hoped he wasn't playing a game with her.

"Thank you, mademoiselle. I will say good night now."

I closed the door and returned to the chaise. I thought of the covenstead in the house. I don't know why, but somehow I was drawn there, and before I knew it. I was traversing the corridor.

The room was lighted, and someone wearing a hooded cloak was kneeling before the altar. Since I had made no attempt to be quiet, the person knew someone had entered the room. However, my heart skipped a beat when the hood slipped down and revealed a bald head. The figure stood up, turned around, and for a moment I thought I was looking at a stranger.

"I was waiting for you to come, Nila." It was my aunt. Without a trace of embarrassment, she raised her arms and slipped the hood back on her head. "Yes, I am bald. But it doesn't present a problem, since I can afford the best wigs. I have a collection of them, and I'm sure you will agree they are beautiful."

"So beautiful I had no idea you weren't wearing your own hair."

She shrugged slightly. "Why not indulge myself?'

"Why not, indeed," I agreed. "However, I don't believe that you willed me to come here. I came of my own accord."

Her smile mocked me. "If that is what you wish to believe, then tell me—just why did you come?"

"I don't know," I admitted.

"You see?" She shrugged.

"I don't see," I said. "Were you practicing witchcraft?"

"I suppose you would call it that. I call it merely exercising my will. Our ceremonies are designed to call upon the powers from the celestial sphere to pass into our bodies."

"If you did send for me, may I ask why?"

"The answer is simple. Stop fighting the fact that you are a witch. You know it. I know it. Everyone here knows it."

"And I suppose everyone in the village knows it."

"We needn't concern ourselves with those peasants."

"Is that how you regard them?"

"They are stupid, ignorant people."

"I thought your good deeds were done out of the kindness of your heart."

She smiled. "I really care nothing about them. Nothing! But so long as I keep them pacified, they may damn me, but they won't burn me."

"Do you fear that?" I asked in surprise.

A shadow crossed her face. "Yes, my child, I do. Too many of our forebears suffered that terrible end."

I understood now the reason for her philanthropy. "Is everyone in this house a witch or warlock?"

"Yes, my dear, including you."

"Has everyone except me been initiated into the coven?"

She nodded. "I am the high priestess, and Giles is the high priest."

"Even Francine?"

"She is my handmaiden. Every high priestess has one."

"Mama knew you were a witch, didn't she?"

"Yes. So was my husband, and so was the aunt who raised your mother and me."

"Was Mama ever a part of *wicca*?"

My aunt smiled. "The name comes easily to you."

"Peter instructed me carefully the other night when he freely admitted to being a warlock."

"He is. I knew it the moment he came into the office of my former attorney."

"You preferred someone as young and inexperienced as Peter to someone with more maturity?"

"Definitely. Especially when he has the gift."

"Auntie, I would like to leave this house," I said. "Will you grant me a small loan so I can support myself until I find employment?"

"It would be a foolish waste of your time and my money. You are like me. I sensed it when you were a child, but I was patient."

"You told me you tried to arrange a reconciliation with Mama when my father drowned. Is that true?"

"Yes. Just as I contacted you when I read of your mama's accident. I couldn't bear the thought of your being alone."

"I would rather be alone than be here. I found the covenstead today."

"And discovered George Ambrus there." My aunt walked into the center of the circle and paused. "You didn't throw that sword, my dear. You willed it thrown to frighten him."

"That isn't true. He knocked me off balance, and it slipped from my hand." I paused and studied her carefully. "How did you know?"

She raised her arm and touched her brow. "I saw it all here."

"It was you who willed the sword to frighten him."

She laughed. "It was good having a little fun with him. I could have pierced him with it. The sniveling coward."

I disputed that. "One needn't be a coward to fear being stabbed."

"Nila, will you please stop fighting it? You can have a good life here. If Matthew Arneil fears your powers, there is always Peter. He's a handsome fellow."

"Very. And I abhor his powers as I do yours."

"You will come around," she said serenely.

I hadn't moved from my place inside the door. "Do Mr. and Mrs. Arneil really believe you are such a gracious lady?"

"Why shouldn't they, when I am? Being a witch doesn't make me malevolent.'

"They are warm, compassionate people. I haven't forgotten how kind they were to us."

"You are also thinking of Matthew Arneil, who laughed at your fears of being a witch," she teased.

"Yes," I admitted solemnly. "He is too decent to believe in such things."

Dorothy Daniels

"I'm glad, for your sake," my aunt said.

"What do you mean?"

"You wouldn't want anything to happen to him, would you?"

I eyed her with dismay. "Are you threatening him—or me?"

"I wouldn't want you to grow too fond of him, dear."

"Why not?"

"I have other plans for you," she said softly. "Plans which include a marriage to Peter."

"I don't love him."

"Do you love Matthew Arneil?"

"I scarcely know him," I said quietly.

"Yet he has left a most favorable impression on you."

"Yes."

"Even though he laughed at your fears of witchcraft."

"Auntie, if you ever call down a curse upon him, I'll . . ."

"You already know the language, my dear. What will you do?"

I felt defeated. "I don't know."

"I doubt I will ever be called upon to do such a thing," she said. "We are having an initiation Sunday night. Do you wish to participate?"

"No," I exclaimed firmly.

"A pity," she said with a sigh. "But as I said, you will come around. You have no choice."

I changed the subject. "When will Peter return?"

"In time for the initiation."

"Who is to be initiated?"

"Why should you be interested when you refuse to attend?"

"I'm just wondering why anyone would be so foolish as to go through a ceremony that will make him a social outcast."

House of Silence

"Many keep their status a secret."

"How many members are in your coven?"

"A full coven numbers thirteen. However, we have initiated well over one hundred here."

"In this room?" I asked.

"No. In the forest covenstead."

"Where did you you get that many members?" I asked scornfully.

"From the inn, my dear. They come here for tea. I give them a tour of the house, and if I feel they have the gift or wish to learn the mysteries of our cult, I invite them back. In every case, they bring up the subject."

"What happens to them afterward? Or is it just a bit of foolishness they indulge in while on vacation?"

"Indeed not. You have seen that book filled with names. The Arneil Inn is famous, and guests come from all over the country. Most of our recruits come from the inn. When they return to their own homes, they start a coven. Sometimes Giles and I travel to them and lend our assistance."

"You are an evil woman," I said quietly.

"You might convince the villagers of that, but they consider you in the same category. As for the Arneils, they would never believe you."

"What you are really saying is that I am trapped here."

"If you wish to put it that way," my aunt said calmly. "You will find true happiness one day—when you become one of us."

"I hate the way you threaten me."

"I would never harm you, my dear."

"What about Matthew Arneil?"

"Just now, I see no reason to use my powers against him."

"Suppose I told him about you?"

"He would laugh at you, just as he did when you told him that we are witches." She paused, but when I remained silent, she continued. "I am an extremely wealthy woman. One day, all I possess will be yours. When that day comes, I want to make certain you carry on my work."

"I don't want your wealth, Auntie. I grew up without money."

"But in a good environment," she reminded me gently. "Thanks to me. I did not tell you everything, nor will I at this moment. I like surprises. Do you?"

"It depends."

"I'm sorry our talk has depressed you. When I summoned you here, I had hoped we would make a little progress." She motioned to the altar. "I wished to tell you about the significance of each object on the altar, and also about *The Book of Shadows*."

"I'm not interested, Auntie," I said. "I wish Mama had known you were supporting us. I also wish Miss Bingham had known how diabolical you are."

"Have I been unkind to you?" she asked. "Haven't I been more than generous?"

"You have tried to buy me," I said. "You are using your wealth in an attempt to seduce me into a life of evil."

"One can do much good with witchcraft. You saved a puppy's life."

"And he wouldn't let me near him."

"That should convince you that you will be unhappy among normal people. We must live apart in order to perform good deeds—and punish those who would destroy us."

"Good night, Auntie."

I turned and left the room. Safely back in my suite, I went to my bedside and dropped to my knees. I tried to pray, but was too terrified. I knew that satanism and witchcraft were not the same, but they were closely aligned. There was an altar in the covenstead, though I had heard no mention of satanism and hoped there was no depravity of that kind practiced here.

I wanted to cry but was too numbed by despair. I must convince Matthew that this house was evil. Perhaps if he saw the covenstead, he would believe me, or at least know it wasn't all in my mind. I would even relate what had happened when George Ambrus was there.

I was sure that I was a prisoner, and that my aunt felt it was only a matter of time before I would weaken. She certainly would not grant me a loan. I believed I had been under her watchful eye since my birth, and Papa's death had made it even easier for her to keep track of me. Miss Bingham would never have guessed the true reason she was given such generous endowments. If she had, she would have refused them and sent Mama and me packing.

SEVEN

My ball gown was elegant, with its rich trimming of lace and pearls. A delicate design of pink chrysanthemum petals was embroidered on the delicate blue background, and a corsage was pinned to the front. A garland of pearls with crystal pendants started on the bosom and curved to the right at the waist, where it was fastened by clasps. Francine parted my hair in the center and drew it back in a coil, ornamenting it with twists of pearls.

"I borrowed these from your aunt," she said as she arranged them in my hair.

"Won't she be using them tonight?"

"She is not going."

"Why not?"

"It is not for me to question my mistress," she replied, still fussing with my hair.

She went into the sitting room and returned with a blue velvet box. "Your aunt wants to give these to you. She asks you to wear them."

I opened the box and saw a beautiful pearl necklace with matching earrings. "These must have cost a fortune," I exclaimed.

Francine laughed. "Your aunt has many fortunes. Let me put the earrings on you."

"I don't wish to wear them," I said.

"You must, mademoiselle. Your aunt wishes to see you before you go. Do not displease her."

"And if I do?" I asked Francine's reflection in the mirror.

"I pay for it, mademoiselle," she said. "Please, have pity."

I put the box down and clipped on the earrings while she fastened the necklace. The door knocker sounded downstairs.

"That is probably Mr. Arneil," she said.

"I hope so. I'm anxious to get to the ball."

"More anxious, I think, to see him." Her mischievous laughter was contagious.

"Yes," I admitted. "I found his company very pleasurable."

"I am happy for you, mademoiselle. But your aunt prefers Peter for you."

"How would you know?" I spoke as I eased my gloves on.

"I know your aunt. She thinks of Peter as a son. He is the most handsome man I have ever seen, next to Giles."

"Giles has the added attraction of maturity."

"I'll go down and tell Mr. Arneil you are ready," Francine said. "It will give me an excuse to look at him."

"Run along."

I looked around the room for a shawl or cloak of some sort. Apparently Francine had forgotten to lay one out. I went into the closet to find a wrap. My hands touched a velvet cloak, and I lifted it off the rod and brought it into the room. It was lined in white satin and had a white, braided belt. I slipped it off the hanger and was about to put it on when I saw the hood. I cried out in dismay. It was a duplicate of what my aunt had been wearing at the covenstead downstairs. I grasped the bedpost as a wave of weakness encompassed me. When I regained my equilibrium, I returned it to the closet. I chose a satin, fringed shawl instead and slipped it over my shoulders as I left the suite.

I reached the head of the stairs and was about to

descend when my aunt called to me. She was standing just outside her sitting room door.

"Didn't Francine tell you I wished to see how you looked?"

"Yes, Auntie." I was filled with distaste at the sight of her, but hoped I was successful at concealing it. "I'm a little late. I forgot."

"Open your shawl and let me see the gown." I obeyed, and she nodded approval. "Enchanting. Have a pleasant evening."

"Thank you. I'm sure I will. I'm sorry you have a headache."

"I survive them. Things will go smoothly for you if you behave."

"Behave?"

"Loyalty, my dear. Loyalty."

"I am giving a lot of thought to the discussion we had last night."

"I'm glad. I was beginning to grow a little concerned."

"Please give me time, Auntie. It's a little unsettling to learn I'm not like others."

"That will change. When it does, come to me."

"I will." I couldn't believe it was I speaking. Yet suddenly I knew I had to play her game so convincingly she would not see through my charade.

She approached me and kissed my cheek. I forced a smile, which she returned with a little nod. I turned and headed for the stairs, fearful she might see the revulsion I had felt when her cold lips touched my cheek.

Downstairs, Francine came forward. "Forgive me, mademoiselle. I forgot to select a wrap. The one you chose is pretty." She gave an almost imperceptible nod and shifted her eyes in the direction of the parlor. "Very manly. And perhaps a little impatient. You'll make a handsome couple."

"Thank you, Francine." I started for the parlor, but

Matthew already stood in the doorway. I felt myself blush as he eyed me with open admiration.

"How did you manage to get such a lovely gown on such short notice?" he asked. He raised my gloved hand to his lips. I dared not glance upstairs, fearful my aunt was there and had observed the gesture. But Francine looked up, then gave me a nod of reassurance. I hoped her friendliness toward me was genuine. I knew she didn't care too much for my aunt, but that she didn't dare reveal her dislike lest my aunt become aware of it.

Matthew escorted me to the buggy. Lamps on either side of the dash illuminated our way.

"Thank you for accompanying me tonight."

"I wanted to see you very much."

"You don't know how good that sounds."

"I'm glad. I must talk to you, though I'm afraid to."

"Afraid of something? Or someone?"

"Both. I just hope you won't laugh at me."

"I promise I won't."

"Will you promise to believe me?"

"What would you want to lie about?"

"It isn't that. It's *wicca*. Witchcraft."

"Don't tell me we're back on that again."

"Yes. I'm afraid even to think about it, lest my aunt find out."

"I thought she was coming. I saw Giles at the inn today, and he said he would be attending the ball tonight."

"That must have been before my aunt's headache."

"No doubt. What is troubling you, Nila?"

"I'm frightened for you as well as for myself."

"I'm becoming more and more mystified. The road widens here. I'm going to pull the carriage over so I can concentrate on what you're saying. Certainly you're unnerved about something."

He guided the horse off to the side of the road and took my hand.

Dorothy Daniels

"You're trembling from head to foot. Tell me what's bothering you. I shan't deride anything you say as I did yesterday. You're much too sensible to be upset about nothing."

I told him about the covenstead in the forest and what had happened when I confronted George Ambrus there. I then related the discussion with my aunt, when she had threatened Matthew.

"She wishes me to marry Peter Rogerson. He is a warlock—and admits to it."

"You mean they actually believe that?" He sounded incredulous.

"You promised not to laugh at anything I said."

His hands tightened around mine. "Im sorry."

"It's all right. My aunt said you wouldn't believe she and I are witches."

He half smiled. "If you are, you're a beautiful one."

"I am a witch, but will never be initiated. However, I realized tonight I must let my aunt believe I am willing. Otherwise, something horrible might happen to you."

"Nila, I'm not belittling you when I say that I am quite capable of taking care of myself."

"This is different. This is evil."

"You aren't evil."

"Not yet. I hope I never succumb."

"You won't. I'll not let your aunt or Giles—or anyone else—exert their evil influence over you."

"Then you believe what I've told you?"

"Yes. I also know you are terribly frightened. Do you want to get out of there?"

"More than anything."

"Then stay at the inn. I can be with you there more easily than if I were driving to your aunt's."

"I don't want you to assume any responsibility for me."

"I'd like to assume a great deal." There was a smile on his face. "You're already very dear to me."

House of Silence

"Aren't you repulsed by what I've told you?"

"I'll admit I don't like witchcraft or satanism or any of those cults. But there is nothing about you that repulses me. You don't have to go back to your aunt's."

"I must. Somehow she knew what I had told you at the inn, and was even aware that you had dismissed it with a laugh. She must not suspect I have told you more."

"What is your greatest fear?"

"That she will harm you."

He bent and kissed my cheek. "My dear Nila, you have completely captured my heart. I love you."

"And I love you," I replied seriously. "I didn't realize it until my aunt uttered her veiled threat, though I was made aware of it tonight as soon as our eyes met."

"Only if I kiss you will you know for certain. I want to marry you."

He gathered me close as his lips covered mine. It was a gentle, lingering kiss.

When he released me, his hands cupped my face. "Do you love me?"

"Yes. Oh, yes, my darling, but I would seal your fate by marrying you."

"My love for you is so strong that nothing—not even evil forces—could destroy it."

"Nonetheless, I must return to my aunt's. She cannot even suspect we are in love."

"That will be difficult to hide—at least for me."

"And for me—but I'll do my best. And now, darling Matthew, let us be on our way. I have never attended such a formal party, and I wish to enter the ballroom on your arm."

"You shall, my beloved. I have already told my parents about you. If you are willing, I would like to court you. I have their full approval."

"I'm glad." I wished I could have been joyous, but I felt our love was hopeless. My aunt was so clever, wily, and skilled in the art of witchcraft that I would never outwit her. Nonetheless, I was thrilled to be with Matthew.

He again slipped his arm around me, and I sat close to him until we reached the village. My problem seemed insurmountable, but I would not let it disturb me tonight. This was my debut, and I wanted to enjoy every moment.

The ballroom was very large, with mirrored panels that reflected the lights. The orchestra had just started a waltz. Matthew's arm enclosed my waist, I rested my hand on his shoulder, and our bodies moved in perfect rhythm to the music. Our eyes met and held as if drawn by a magnet. As far as we were concerned, there was no one else on the dance floor. Our love had shut out the world, and I had never known such happiness.

But it was short-lived. A voice behind me spoke my name. I looked over my shoulder and saw Giles Lazarno, who smiled at my astonishment. I gasped aloud when I saw his partner was none other than Miss Bingham.

She said, "Good evening, Nila," and smiled serenely.

I managed to return the greeting, but missed a step and stumbled against Matthew. He greeted Giles, nodded to Miss Bingham, and looked down at me, raising his brows questioningly.

"Please take me someplace where it's quiet," I murmured.

He sensed my uneasiness and guided me to the side of the ballroom. He escorted me through a door leading onto the side porch. We went down the steps and continued on across the lawn until we came to a cast-iron settee.

"What's wrong?" he asked when we were finally seated.

"Miss Bingham, Giles's dancing partner."

"What about her?"

"She runs the school where Mama and I lived. I

don't know what she is doing here. At least, I hope I don't."

"She is a guest here. I saw her registering at the desk this morning."

"I wasn't aware that Giles knew her."

"If your aunt does, we may assume Giles does also."

I nodded. "I suppose he would have met her through the years."

"What did you mean when you said you hoped you didn't know the reason for her being here?"

"I told you there is going to be an initiation."

"Yes."

"I wondered who it might be. I never dreamed it would be Miss Bingham."

"You don't know that it is," Matthew cautioned. "She could be perfectly innocent."

"Yes." I pressed a hand against my brow. "I'm becoming too obsessed with witchcraft."

"We can sit here awhile. In fact, I like it better being alone with you."

"We must go back." I was already on my feet. "I promise to be good. It was foolish of me to get upset."

"Just why must we go back?" Matthew got to his feet reluctantly.

I dared not tell him that I feared Giles, so I said, "It's such a beautiful ball, and I want to dance."

"Then we shall."

Matthew caught my hand as we moved across the lawn. We had just entered the hall when Giles came toward us. He was carrying the still form of a woman in his arms.

I thought it was Miss Bingham until I heard Matthew say, "Mother!" in a voice of alarm. "This way, Giles," he added and moved briskly down the hall to a suite. Giles carried Mrs. Arneil to a couch and gently laid her on it.

"What happened?" Matthew asked, already at his mother's side.

"She complained of dizziness," Giles said, "then collapsed while we were dancing."

"I should know better at my age," she said softly. She opened her eyes, then closed them quickly against the light.

"I'll get the doctor," Matthew said. "Please stay, Giles."

"I will," he replied, his tone solicitous.

I knelt beside the couch. "What happened, Mrs. Arneil? I am Nila Parris."

"I know, my dear. I recognized your soft voice."

"Please tell me what happened," I urged.

"I had a sudden, uncontrollable urge to laugh while dancing with Giles—just to open my mouth and laugh like a fool. I tried not to give in to it, for I didn't want to make a spectacle of myself."

"Perhaps it was something humorous Giles said."

"We weren't conversing," she replied.

I looked up at Giles, who was regarding me with a hint of ridicule in his features.

"Did you give in to it, Mrs. Arneil?" I persisted in my questioning.

"No. But I became very dizzy. I couldn't control my body and started to fall like a rag doll. My legs suddenly refused to support me, and I collapsed. It was most embarrassing."

"Do you still feel dizzy?"

She opened her eyes to a mere slit, but grasped the edge of the couch as if she feared falling off.

"Yes," she said. "It's horrible."

I stood up, walked behind the couch, and touched her brow. "I am going to see if I can make the dizziness go away. Just lie quietly and don't talk. In a few minutes you will be yourself."

I looked down at her face, still slack from the attack of vertigo. Her body gave a convulsive jerk, and my eyes shifted momentarily to Giles. His attention was fixed on Mrs. Arneil. I knew he was responsible for

House of Silence

what had happened to her, just as I knew he was fighting me now—trying to prolong the spell he had cast on her.

For the first time, I was going to test my power. Would it be stronger than his? I no longer fought the fearful possibility of being a witch. I was. Giles had cast a spell on this dear lady, and I must break it.

She gave another convulsive shudder, and I looked down at her. My hands covered her head while my mind commanded her to relax. I was trying to tell her that she must not let anyone force her to do something against her will.

I don't know how long I stood over her, calling on my powers and hoping they were stronger than Giles's. Gradually, Mrs. Arneil's body quieted. I did not relax for a moment, fearful that Giles's powers would once again possess her.

Her eyes opened slowly. "I feel better, Nila. I really do."

"You'll be all right now," I said, taking my hands from her head.

"I must sit up." She even managed a smile.

"Let me help you," Giles said, slipping an arm around her shoulders.

"No, Giles," I said quietly. "I will help Mrs. Arneil. You go back to the ball. You didn't come alone, did you?"

"Yes," he smiled, stepping back, acknowledging defeat. "It was your aunt who invited Miss Bingham. She arrived late last night. Tomorrow Peter will call for her here and take her to your aunt's house."

"I see," I said quietly.

"I'm sure you do," he replied. "Oh—I must compliment you on your ministrations to Mrs. Arneil."

I was seated on the couch beside her. She seemed completely recovered.

"I'm so sorry, Giles," she said, looking up at him. "I hope I didn't embarrass you."

"Not in the least, Mrs. Arneil. I'll excuse myself now and let you rest."

"I should know better than to dance every dance," she replied, making light of what had happened. "But I do love it so."

"I enjoyed dancing with you, Mrs. Arneil. Good night and rest well."

"Thank you, Giles." She turned to me. "I must stand up so Matthew won't worry when he returns with the doctor."

She stood, not allowing me to assist her as she walked about the room. "You see?" she smiled. "Whatever you did, Nila, it worked."

"You were tense and very frightened, which was only natural."

"I'd never experienced such a strange feeling."

"You probably never will again," I said.

Just then Matthew arrived with the doctor. Matthew looked pleasantly surprised to see his mother standing in the center of the room.

"You shouldn't have bothered Dr. Hebert. My son worries about me too much, Doctor."

"With the symptoms he described, he had a right to," Dr. Hebert said. "However, you look quite fit at the moment."

"I am," she said. "I don't know what Nila did, but it worked."

I avoided Matthew's intense gaze. I was frightened of losing him. I sensed that for the first time he believed everything I had told him. He knew that I had helped his mother.

As we returned to the ball, Matthew said, "I think you deserve a glass of champagne."

"I would like some," I said gratefully.

"Do you wish to go outside, or sit and watch the dancing?"

Matthew motioned to a waiter carrying a tray of

champagne glasses. We entered the ballroom, sipping our champagne.

"Giles seems quite attentive to Miss Bingham," Matthew observed.

"Yes."

They were in the center of the dance floor, unaware of anyone else. Francine came to mind, and I wondered what she would think if she saw how entranced they were with each other. Miss Bingham's flushed face made her look younger and more attractive.

"You know what happened to your mother, don't you?" I asked, turning to Matthew.

"Yes. Giles cast a spell."

"He tried to prolong it while you were out. For the first time, I worked my magic and found it stronger than his. I wonder what he will tell my aunt."

"I wish you wouldn't go back there."

"I must. To be truthful, it isn't so difficult now that you know I'm speaking the truth."

"I no longer have any doubt. I am going to study witchcraft and see what makes one a witch, and if you can escape its wickedness."

"I wish you luck. I am still wondering—though it seems insane—if Miss Bingham is to be initiated into the coven tomorrow night."

"Were you invited?"

"Yes, but I refused to go."

"Where is it going to be?"

"In the forest covenstead."

"In the morning we must meet nearby and observe the proceedings."

"What if they find us?"

He smiled as he spoke. "We must exert your powers to make certain they don't."

"Where will we meet?"

"Describe the area."

After I did, he said, "Do you have any way of

knowing when they leave the house, so you can follow and meet me?"

"I have a perfect view from my window of the path leading into the forest."

"I will watch from the forest. When they have left, I will meet you at the path, and we will follow them to the covenstead."

Our attention was diverted by the flickering lamps. The six chandeliers hanging from the ceiling began to swing back and forth mysteriously. Some of the ladies screamed at the phenomenon, and the gentlemen tried to escort them from the room. Someone brushed against us, knocking the glasses from our hands.

Matthew said, "Don't move. We're safe here away from that crowd."

A few ladies fell, and some gentlemen rushed to assist them to their feet. During this commotion, the orchestra—to their credit—continued to play. I looked toward the far end of the ballroom and saw Giles and Miss Bingham regarding the scene with amusement.

I turned to Matthew. There was no need to speak. He had seen them and was as shocked as I. Just as the room cleared, the chandeliers slowed their swaying. The lamplight steadied and became bright again; however, the magic of the evening was gone.

"Must I take you back to that house?" he asked.

"Yes. If for no other reason than that I want to know just how involved Miss Bingham is with that group."

"I do so with great reluctance," he said.

"Could you explain to your parents why I was staying here?" I asked. "Do you think they would approve of your marrying a witch?"

"I would marry you anyway," he replied firmly. "I love you."

I stood up. "At least I had this night. Apparently Giles was sent here to create mischief, but I bested him. You should see that your mother is comfortable."

Matthew knew better than to argue. He excused himself and returned with my wrap. He assured me his mother was not quite herself, adding that she sent her thanks.

I made no comment. Matthew understood my silence as we approached the buggy. Before urging the horse into motion, he slipped an arm around my waist, drew me close, and kissed me with even greater fervor than before. I was fearful Giles might see us, and pushed him away gently, yet I was breathless and weak with emotion. I wondered if I should accept Matthew's proposal of marriage. Could the bond of love between us be strong enough to wipe out the evil within me? I rested my head against his shoulder during the drive home. He bent his head slightly and kissed my brow.

"I love you, darling," he said softly. "Dream of that instead of witches and warlocks."

"That's what I'm doing," I said wistfully. "You have made me feel very special."

"You are and always will be. We'll marry very soon. Promise?"

"I promise." I was playing a game. I knew I couldn't.

The next instant, the mood was broken by his exclamation of dismay.

"That red glow in the sky," he said pointing. "Looks like a house is on fire. Hold on to me. This horse is going to run."

To my dismay, we turned down the street where Mrs. Ambrus and George lived. It was my turn to gasp when I saw their home fully engulfed in flames.

A crowd was gathering, but it would have been a futile gesture to form a bucket brigade. The house looked as if it had exploded.

Matthew halted the horse, vaulted the gate, and ran close to the house. I looked around, trying to catch sight of Mrs. Ambrus. The flames illuminated the entire area with their macabre light. I was terrified and remembered what my aunt had said about her fear of being burned.

"Has anyone seen Mrs. Ambrus or George?" Matthew had to shout to be heard above the crackling of the flames and the crashing sound of the falling structure.

Hopelessness showed on everyone's blank face. Then a man's agonized cry pierced the night, and I turned to see George Ambrus running toward the house. He ran through the gate and didn't stop until the flames threatened to engulf him.

Matthew went over to him and said something. His features hardened as he looked at Matthew, then he turned toward the carriage. I was fully visible, leaning out of the carriage, hoping desperately that Mrs. Ambrus might have escaped the blaze.

George walked toward the carriage, raised his arm, and pointed an accusing finger at me. "The witch. The young witch, Mrs. Dunbar's niece. She started the fire. She burned my mother to death. She did it." He picked up a large stone and threw it at me. It bounced off the dash and grazed my wrist.

Now everyone's attention switched from the fire to me. I moved back into the seat, wondering if the hostile crowd would turn on me.

"So she's the one," a male voice commented. "We don't want any more o' them here."

His statement was followed by another stone, which struck the top of the carriage. The horse became nervous as people shouted and gathered around the carriage.

I closed my eyes and sat far back in the seat as an avalanche of stones struck the carriage. A pain shot through the length of my leg when one of them hit my knee. I felt the carriage move as someone got into it and braced myself, believing I was going to be abducted.

House of Silence

Fortunately it was Matthew. "I'll get you out of here. George is stirring up that crowd."

I was too filled with terror to answer. The carriage was already moving at a good clip. Matthew guided the animal into a field.

Finally we were back on the road, and Matthew emitted an audible "Whew," adding, "I should never have left you. I had no idea the villagers hated your aunt so vehemently."

"Perhaps they have a good reason," I said. "I'm wondering if my aunt caused this fire tonight, or if Giles worked some of his black magic."

"I don't know, but it's a rotten business," Matthew reasoned. "Darling, I cannot bring you back to that house."

"I am safer there than at the inn," I replied. "It would be dreadful if the villagers learned I was living there and came after me to try and burn me at the stake."

"Don't talk that way."

"I can't help it. I have my aunt's fear of being burned. Many of our ancestors suffered that fate."

"I never gave credence to witchcraft before," Matthew said firmly. "To me, it was ignorant foolishness."

"Do you still think that?" I asked.

"No," he admitted reluctantly. "It's unfortunate George has turned the villagers against you."

"Did you speak to him about a job?" I asked.

"No. I went to his house twice, but he wasn't there. Come to think of it, his mother said he was investigating evil. At the time I didn't know about the covenstead and thought she was ill and not quite right in her mind."

"I wonder if he went back there. He broke the latch on the door in his haste to escape. Not that I blame him, since the sword embedded itself in the door six inches from his back."

"Please don't ask me to hire him, Nila. After what I

witnessed, I fear for your safety. I wonder if they'll form a vigilante group and storm your aunt's mansion."

"They fear her powers too much. That is why I am safe there."

"I can see the logic in that," Matthew said thoughtfully. "At least for the time being. Don't leave the estate tomorrow, please."

"I won't. Will you come tomorrow night?"

"Most definitely. I shall explore the area tomorrow afternoon and wait for you in the evening."

"You'll need food."

"I'll bring a sandwich and some fruit. I'm going back to the remains of the Ambrus residence. Mrs. Ambrus's body has to be removed when the fire cools."

"If there's anything left. My aunt will probably pay the burial expenses."

"No," he replied. "I will. It's about time the villagers stopped taking from your aunt. They'll accept gratuities from the witch, and after tonight, they may burn her."

"Oh, Matthew, what is going to happen?" I asked fearfully.

"We're going to put an end to all of this," he replied quietly. "I don't know how or when, but I'll find a way. This can't go on. I love you, and I'm going to get you out of this."

"I'm puzzled about Giles's attentions to Miss Bingham. Francine is in love with him, though I'm not certain he is with her. I'm beginning to think he is a rogue."

"What makes you say that about him?"

"It's difficult to explain. I believe Giles cast that spell on your mother on my aunt's orders. She knows about us, and she has other plans for me."

"Marriage?"

I nodded. "Peter Rogerson. Giles told me tonight

Peter will arrive at the house tomorrow with Miss Bingham."

"When did he tell you that?"

"While you went for the doctor. Now you know why I'm frightened for you."

"Don't be. As I told you before, I'm quite capable of taking care of myself. Now, what do you know about Francine and Giles?"

I told him about the night I had decided to visit the covenstead in my aunt's home and had observed Francine and Giles arguing about his initiating Miss some-one-or-other. I finally told him that Francine had been nude beneath her robe.

"Had she and Giles performed some sort of ceremony that night?"

"I don't know. They were barefoot. I know they are lovers because Francine went with him to his room."

"What a dreadful place," Matthew said grimly. "I'm getting you out of there at the earliest opportunity."

"Don't worry about me," I said.

"How can I avoid it?" he asked impatiently.

"You forget that I am a witch also. I have powers."

We turned into the drive. We ceased our conversation for fear that someone might overhear, even though I knew my aunt had such great mental perception that she didn't need to be present to know what was going on.

He escorted me into the dimly lit hall. I gave a slight negative shake of my head when he raised his arms to embrace me. I extended a hand. "Good night, Matthew."

"May I see you again?"

"I will invite you for tea."

"Be assured I shall accept. Good night."

He closed the door, and I went directly upstairs. I felt certain Giles hadn't returned. He was probably still watching the fire.

EIGHT

I slept fitfully as I dreamed about the terror that filled this house. I could not escape becoming part of it while I lived here. By the same token, I could not leave and expose Matthew to their bedevilment. I had neglected to tell him that my aunt and Giles had initiated several guests at the inn. I was glad I hadn't, as he was already too concerned by my presence here—especially after seeing the black magic Giles had worked on his mother.

It was after nine o'clock when I went down to breakfast. I fully expected to eat alone, but my aunt was seated at the table with a cup of coffee.

We greeted each other cordially. I helped myself to the food on the serving table, then sat down opposite her.

"Did you have a pleasant evening, my dear?" My aunt opened the conversation as I concentrated on the food.

"I'm certain you know what kind of evening it was." I spread marmalade on my roll as I spoke, pleased that my manner was as casual as hers.

"How could I when I wasn't there?" Her air of innocence disgusted me.

"Even if you couldn't, Giles could have informed you."

"I haven't seen Giles."

"I think you're lying to me," I said.

"Now you're being cruel, Nila."

"Stop playing cat and mouse, Auntie," I said coldly.

She sighed. "Very well. You didn't have a pleasant evening. You found Matthew Arneil a bore and something less than a gentleman."

"That isn't true. I love him." I gasped after the words came out. I had never meant to admit that. Her knowledge of our love would endanger him.

My aunt smiled triumphantly. She knew she had bested me. "My dear, that is quite impossible. You're a witch. You proved it last night by exerting greater power than Giles. Our power is great. Giles displayed it by making the chandeliers sway. That was amusing, wasn't it?"

"It was horrifying."

"So Giles said."

"Then you admit you talked with him."

"Yes." She smiled reminiscently. "And I was in the parlor when you and Matthew returned. I could view you both, and I saw you discourage Matthew from embracing you."

"Is there anything you don't know?" I asked in despair.

"Very little."

The conversation quickly made me lose my appetite. I sipped coffee.

"What part does Miss Bingham play in your little game?"

"It isn't a game, Nila. *Wicca* plays a very serious role in my life."

"I consider it very wicked."

"As I have already told you, one day you'll see it my way. Once you do, you'll be a much happier young lady. As for Miss Bingham, I was rude to her when she told me she would not allow you to remain at the school. So I invited her to visit me."

I set my coffee cup down and looked directly at her. "I do not believe you. You have been lying to me from the moment of our first meeting."

"Please, Nila. Your mother was my sister. I watched over you both after your father's death."

"I wish you hadn't," I said flatly. "I feel sorry for Miss Bingham. She has no more idea than I of what she is walking into. Or does she?"

My aunt's smile was knowing.

"Of course she does," I exclaimed. "She enjoyed the terror of the guests last night as much as Giles. They were both smiling like idiots."

"Giles did very well."

"Was Giles instrumental in Mrs. Ambrus's death?"

"He was there, but he had used up his powers. As I already told you, we have to practice our ceremonial rites to conjure up our supernatural powers."

"Who set the torch to the Ambrus house?"

"Pierce, though Miss Bingham thinks she was instrumental in doing so."

"I studied all the faces there, expecting to see Giles."

"He kept out of sight, but saw you being stoned. I was sorry about that, but we are not treated kindly here. Despite that, I will pay for Mrs. Ambrus's funeral."

"You should, though Matthew told me last night he would undertake that responsibility."

"That is kind of him, though foolish, since George stoned you."

"I can understand his anger."

"Back to Miss Bingham," my aunt said. "I may as well tell you that I have purchased her school."

"Why?" I exclaimed in dismay.

"We need young recruits, my dear," she said reflectively. "Miss Bingham has the perfect setting for us. Many may have the gift, and even if some do not, they may be willing for the thrill of it. Young people love to be daring."

"You are wicked, Auntie," I said, shocked at this latest revelation.

"Dedicated is the proper word. I have more to tell you. Giles and Clare Bingham are going to wed. You know how handsome he is."

"Yes—just as I know how plain Miss Bingham is. He doesn't love her."

"That's not important. She is mad about him."

"Most spinsters her age would be mad over any man."

"The girls will be enchanted by him."

"He is a seducer." I made no attempt to hide my disgust.

"Yes. He even seduced me at one time. Our relationship now is of a strictly friendly nature."

"Do you trust him?"

"Of course not. He makes my sleeping potions much too strong. I don't always take them, but he doesn't know that. Nor does Francine. I don't mind her having a close relationship with him. It keeps her docile."

"With her, it may not be just an affair."

"Has she spoken to you about him?"

"She is very loyal to you."

"As my handmaiden she had better be. But she is not completely loyal. I do not approve of improper relationships."

"When you yourself have been guilty?"

"He is closer to my age. However, he will live at the school when he and Miss Bingham marry."

"Are you doing this to punish Francine?"

"Of course not. I am not interested in how she feels."

"You are heartless."

"I'm only doing my duty." She turned and glanced at a gold clock on the mantel. "Miss Bingham will arrive this afternoon with Peter."

"Giles told me," I said with little interest.

"I will expect you to be gracious to Peter."

"I am gracious to everyone."

"I mean more than that." She studied her highly

Dorothy Daniels

buffed nails as she spoke. "The next marriage will be between you and Peter."

"No, Auntie. I will marry only for love. I do not love Peter."

"He is quite taken with you, and he certainly is attractive."

"I wouldn't marry a man because of his looks."

"For what, then?"

"His character."

Her low, throaty laughter held a sinister note. "Peter's business acumen has no equal."

"I suppose so, when he uses his powers of witchcraft to win cases and consummate business deals."

My aunt suppressed a yawn. "My dear, you have wearied me. I wanted a pleasant discussion, and you have turned my every statement into something ugly."

"Every one of your schemes is ugly."

"Very well." She stood, then looked down at me. "I will say one thing more. There will be an initiation tonight. The official robe is in your closet, and you are to wear nothing beneath it."

She paused, but when I made no answer she continued. "Anyway, should you wish to come tell Francine, and she will escort you. I am sure you studied the book of names and know that Pierce and Dulcy have been loyal members for years. They were instrumental in getting many members in New York City. They served me well there. I want them with me now so that when the school opens, they can assist with the new initiates. You and Peter will also be present. You really have no choice, like it or not. That is, if you truly love Matthew."

"You wouldn't harm him," I exclaimed, unable to hide my fear.

"I have already told you I am very dedicated. I will allow no one to stand in my way. I didn't count on him when I brought you up here. I should have known better than to take you to the inn. I hadn't been there in

120

some time. I detest the Arneils' plan to build an inn across the lake."

"I should think you would like it, Auntie," I said caustically. "You may gain new recruits."

"Be assured I shall. Miss Bingham will arrive at two, and tea will be served at three on the veranda."

If I had thought to anger her, I had failed. However, she had revealed that I meant little to her—other than having been brought here to learn the ways of *wicca*. I couldn't believe that witches performed good deeds.

Yet I had with Mrs. Arneil, and with the puppy. However, the incident at the inn wasn't the result of goodness. I was glad my aunt had admitted that she caused the sword to flash through the air, and that I had had nothing to do with it. I wondered if she had meant only to frighten George—or to kill him.

The more I thought of these events, the more frightened I became—for myself, and for Matthew. I couldn't keep Matthew out of my mind, and I wondered if he had found the covenstead. My aunt was aware of the fact that Matthew and I had declared our love for each other, and that he would not dismiss my disappearance lightly. I wondered if there was some way in which I could combat the evil forces in this house. I wanted to leave, but would fear for Matthew's safety if I did.

I was dressed for tea when Francine came in later. I needed only to look at her grim expression to know she was aware of my aunt's plans for Giles.

"I am sorry to be late, mademoiselle. I had to attend to Miss Bingham. If you think your aunt buys you pretty clothes, you should see what she bought that foolish woman."

"She looked lovely last night at the ball," I said.

Francine nodded. 'Giles is a fool, but Miss Bingham is a bigger one."

"You needn't play games with me, Francine. I know

why my aunt brought me here. She wishes me to be a part of the coven and learn the ceremonies."

"It is good to know. But I think your aunt went too far when she bought that school. She will get in trouble, seeking out those with the gift. Some may pretend to have it and will come, then go back and talk. The police will find out."

"I would tell the police if I could," I said. "I will not, under any circumstances, be a part of witchcraft. I discovered my power was stronger than Giles's last night when he played a cruel trick on Mrs. Arneil."

"Very well, mademoiselle. I'll tell you what I know. I like you. I do not like the other one. You know why?"

"Yes. But I must tell you I do not like Giles. He is as evil as my aunt."

She nodded. "I was a fool. He will make a bigger fool of that woman your aunt says he must marry."

"Doesn't he want to?"

"He'd do anything to stay here."

"But he won't be here."

"I know. He will live at the school. He will like that also, with all the young girls. I hope they see through him."

"Surely my aunt wouldn't permit infidelity."

Her smile was bitter. "Once I was a nice young lady. Your aunt and Giles came to Paris to see a doctor about her headaches. I will tell you the truth about her headaches. They are really bad, and she suffers. Lately, they've gotten worse. I think maybe something is wrong in her head."

"I don't doubt it, Francine."

"Anyway, I had noticed I could make people do things, and they didn't know it. But nothing bad. I like people."

"How did you meet my aunt?"

She smiled. "I was in a park wheeling a baby carriage for the family I worked for. She and Giles were strolling, and I made Giles's hat blow off and sit on a bush. Then I made you aunt's parasol fly from her hand and join the hat on the bush."

I couldn't help but laugh. "That must have startled them."

"*Oui,* because they had not noticed me. I noticed Giles because he is so handsome. I'll be honest. That is why I am here. He went to my heart the moment I saw him."

"Tell me what happened."

"They looked around and saw me. Giles laughed at once. Then your aunt realized I am like them. She came and talked to me and offered me good money to be her handmaiden. I was initiated into the coven when I returned here with them."

"By Giles, of course."

She lowered her eyes. "*Oui,* mademoiselle. I love him. But your aunt would not allow marriage."

"Did you discuss it with her?"

"She does not know about us."

"She knows, Francine. She told me she doesn't mind, so long as you stay here."

Francine's astonishment at my revelation was not pretense. "Does Giles know that?"

"I doubt it. She likes to play her little games. Perhaps you had better not tell him. She might conjure up something unpleasant for you."

"She would. I must not let her see how hurt I am by having to serve that stupid woman."

"Francine, you are wiser than she gives you credit for."

"I am stupid, mademoiselle. I should have remained in Paris. I was happy enough there. Since you came, I feel shameful."

"I have refused to go to the initiation ceremonies tonight."

"You are a lady. Do not go. But be careful, mademoiselle. Your aunt is evil."

"I believe that."

"You wish to know how evil?"

"That's a strange question."

"I will tell you because I have a bad feeling inside me. Without knowing why, I am frightened. I want to do something good. Maybe I am foolish, but I am worried."

"So am I, Francine. You know I am a witch, just like you."

"You are not evil. Your aunt . . ." Her voice broke off, but she nodded. "Now I'll tell you the horrible thing she did. She made your mother walk off that sidewalk."

"Oh, no!" I exclaimed, horrified by the statement. "Mama was her sister."

"She hated her sister because she was not a witch. The aunt who raised them also hated your mama. That is why your mother did not recognize her sister. They were mean to her while she was growing up. The aunt is a witch also."

I sat down and covered my face with my hands. "Before Mama died, she said she should not have done such a stupid thing."

"She would not have. Your aunt and Pierce followed you both in a carriage. When the beer van was alongside you and your mama, she commanded her to step off curb."

I was too horrified to speak.

"Your aunt laughed when your mama told you your papa was strong."

"Yes," I exclaimed, looking up at Francine. "Mama said he was strong and should not have drowned. Now I know my aunt was responsible for his death."

Francine nodded. "She schemed for the day when she would have you. Now you know the truth, mademoiselle. At least I hope I've done some good. I do not want to be part of the ceremonies anymore. I'll stay away from Giles. But I must be careful. He is like your aunt. *Wicca* is his life."

"Is Miss Bingham a witch?"

Francine shrugged. "Who knows? She has the school. Your aunt kept track of you all these years. She paid Miss Bingham well. Also, she saw to it your mama was paid very little. Your aunt hated your mama and now you. You're in danger. Mr. Arneil should take you away with him."

"He wants to, Francine. We wish to marry. But I fear what she will do to him if I leave here."

She nodded slow agreement, her features somber. "I must go now. I had to tell you the truth. I'll go back to France the first chance I get."

"Matthew and I will help you," I said.

"Thank you." She managed a smile. "You are a very dear young lady. I liked you from the moment I saw you. I did not know your aunt's plan for your mama. It's too late now."

"Too late for Mama," I said. "But not for you and me."

"We will hope."

"Will you go to the initiation tonight?" I asked.

"I hate to, but I must. I am her handmaiden. She will get suspicious if I pretend illness."

"Where is the veranda?" I asked.

"Outside the library."

"Thank you, Francine."

I found it easily enough. Miss Bingham and my aunt were already there with Giles and Peter. Peter came forward and kissed my hand.

"You look charming, Nila," he said. "Miss Bingham has been telling us what a brilliant student you were."

"That is kind of her. I am surprised to find you here, Miss Bingham."

"I would like you to call me Clare, my dear," she said. "You are quite the young lady now. I admired you last night. You danced beautifully."

"Thank you. It was quite a game you and my aunt played with Mama, wasn't it?"

She regarded me benevolently. "Your aunt had your best interests at heart."

"I am sure she did."

My aunt elaborated. "I left nothing to chance. We just told Peter about the affair last night."

"Including Mrs. Ambrus being burned to death? At least, I imagine she was too ill to even leave her bed."

"I'm sorry to say she died," Peter said. "Clare said it was all anyone at the inn talked about."

"It probably took their minds off the swaying chandeliers," I said.

"I think we should pick a more cheerful subject," my aunt said. She was already pouring the tea. "Pass the napkins, Nila, then you may give Clare and the gentlemen their teacups."

"I will be glad to do that, Auntie," I said. Miss Bingham, Peter, and Giles sat down while I served them.

Miss Bingham said, "Giles was kind enough to give me a tour of the rooms where the priceless treasures are kept. I have never seen so much artwork under the roof of one house."

"I took Nila on a tour," Peter said.

"Did you enjoy it, my dear?" my aunt asked.

"Every normal individual admires beauty," I said. "But it seems selfish for so few to see it."

"It does indeed," my aunt agreed. "Peter knows I have already made a provision in my will that the pieces are either to go to a museum or the mansion itself will be turned into a museum. The grounds are so vast that people would enjoy a picnic here."

"Would you allow that, Auntie?" I asked in surprise.

"Certainly," she replied graciously. "I agree with you, Nila. There is much beauty hidden here that we should share."

"Why not now, Auntie?" I asked.

"I must have quiet. It may seem selfish, but these dreadful headaches are so agonizing that sometimes even the chirp of a bird can be unbearable."

"Giles told me that you have been to many doctors. Hasn't one of them been able to give you the slightest relief?"

"No," she replied. "I am being very quiet today, so as not to do anything that would interfere with tonight's initiation. A pity you won't be a part of it, Nila."

"It seems indecent to me," I said.

"That is all in your mind, my dear," Miss Bingham said. "I am eager to be a member of the coven."

"Are you familiar with the ceremonies?"

"Your aunt's handmaiden brought me there this morning and taught me about each step of the initiation ceremony."

"I notice you are not using your cane," I said.

"That was an affectation. I felt it gave me a touch of dignity."

"It did," I agreed. "It also puzzled us, because we could not see the slightest need for it."

And so the time passed with light, inane conversation. I wondered how I could sit here, apparently relaxed and enjoying myself, when I despised every individual in the room—especially my aunt. I now knew that she would not have the slightest compunction in hastening my end, should it suit her.

Her manner toward me was now demeaning, and had lost the warm cordiality so evident when I first arrived. It was all I could do to be civil to this murderess. Yet I could not let her know what Francine had revealed.

Finally my aunt—to my relief—suggested we retire for a rest. I was shaken when Miss Bingham requested Giles to take her for a walk on the grounds. When he asked if she would like to visit the covenstead, she told him that Francine had instructed her very well and she need not go there again until the ceremony. She said she felt like a bride. A bride of Satan, I mused.

Giles's arm went around her waist, and they exchanged knowing glances. I knew they were thinking of the imminent wedding. At least she was. Thank goodness Francine was resigned to it.

I was grateful for the high standards Mama had set for me, and that I had developed strength of character. My aunt had thought to bribe me with gorgeous gowns, beautiful jewelry, and the luxury of living in this evil mansion. My sympathies were entirely with the villagers.

My aunt, Miss Bingham, and Giles had already left the room. I was suddenly conscious of Peter standing near me. He bent and took the teacup from my hand.

"Would you care to go for a walk, Nila?" he asked.

"Ordinarily, yes. But I slept little last night."

"Upset by what happened at the ball?"

"More so by Mrs. Ambrus's death."

"An unfortunate accident. She probably dropped a lamp or was careless with matches."

"Is that what you think happened?" I asked, my manner as innocent as his.

"What else?" he asked. "Don't dwell on it. She didn't have long to live anyway. You saw her hollow cheeks and gray skin."

"That's what makes it so horrible," I said. "To be so ill and have such a ghastly end. She should have died in her sleep."

"It is sad, especially after your aunt made such a generous gesture."

I was tired of his game. Apparently he wasn't aware that my aunt had informed me of her responsibility for the fire. I let him walk to the foot of the stairs with me, then excused myself.

NINE

At five, Francine served dinner in my suite. I was relieved, for I had no desire to mingle with those people.

"It is done that way, mademoiselle," she said. "We are supposed to meditate on the ceremony. So we eat lightly until afterward, when we feast."

"I am not going to the initiation, Francine. And I'm relieved I do not have to dine with that pitiful Miss Bingham."

"More pitiful when she marries Giles. He cannot be faithful to any woman."

"Your spirits seem higher than they were earlier today."

"I feel free," she said, smiling. "I know now I was part of an evil force. I want to go home to Paris. I want goodness. I am still young."

"You might meet a nice gentleman and fall in love."

"Like you, I would still be a witch," she said sadly. "I do not know how to break away."

"Nor do I," I said. "There must be a way."

"If you find it, please tell me."

"I promise."

"Now I must go and prepare Miss Bingham for the ceremony. Your aunt said I am to tell you that, should you change your mind, you have the proper garment."

"I know. But I won't be present."

"I envy your courage. Your aunt is strong and vindictive."

"I'll risk her anger."

I was impatient for darkness, so that I might watch them head for the coven and go meet Matthew. When Dulcy came for my empty tray, she said, "Miss Nila, I will bathe and prepare you for the ceremony, should you wish to be a part of it."

"I have already informed my aunt I will not attend."

"She knows that, but she asked that I attempt to persuade you to change your mind. She would like you to be her handmaiden."

"Doesn't Francine hold that honor?"

"She would have to step aside. Peter is also anxious for you to be the next member of our coven."

"Please tell my aunt I will not be attending."

"I will do that, Miss Nila," she said serenely.

I called to her as she turned to leave the room. "How can you be so proud of having a husband who set a torch to Mrs. Ambrus's home and burned her to death?"

She regarded me with surprise. "He didn't even strike a match, just used his power. Mrs. Ambrus hated you and so does her son."

"He has reason to," I said.

"Your aunt will take care of him in good time," she said.

"You misunderstand me. I don't resent George Ambrus."

"That doesn't matter. Your aunt does."

I nodded, resigned to defeat. Yet I must tell Matthew so he could warn George. The man's bitterness was justified after what my aunt had done.

"Your aunt has ordered me to lay out the robe for the ceremony," Dulcy said.

"It would be a useless gesture," I stated simply.

"Please let me, Miss Nila." I could see she was actually afraid of not following the order.

"Very well." I motioned her to the bedroom.

"Thank you, Miss Nila," Dulcy said as she passed

House of Silence

through the sitting room. I nodded but didn't look up, not wishing to prolong her stay. I was revolted by the lot of them—except Francine, who wanted no further part of this life.

I remained in my suite until darkness fell. The quiet of the place could drive me mad, but I knew it was due to my aunt's severe headaches.

It was nine o'clock before the first figures appeared on the lawn, who I judged to be Dulcy and Pierce. They wore robes identical to the one which still lay on my bed. Without the moon I couldn't see their faces, and the heavy clouds increased the darkness. My eyes grew accustomed to the gloom, though it was perhaps fifteen minutes before I saw a third figure.

He was wearing the hood, and from his firm, springy gait, I gathered it was Peter. Next came my aunt with Francine. My sympathies were aroused at the sight of her. She feared my aunt with good reason. She had caused the death of both my parents, and had been responsible for all kinds of evil deeds in the village. She despised all the villagers, for they knew what she was. They would accept her favors, but would not be beholden to her. They somehow knew the extent of her evil.

Finally Giles and Miss Bingham came into view. Her hood had slipped free of her head. She was blindfolded, and her hands were tied behind her back. I assumed that they were nude beneath the robes. Miss Bingham was having a problem walking, and Giles had an arm about her waist. Their progress was slow, and I didn't move from the window until I saw them disappear beneath the arbor.

I had put on my black dress, which I knew would blend in well with the darkness. I descended the stairs and ran down the hallway. I was anxious to reach Matthew, and I moved rapidly around the house to the rear, heading for the path to the arbor.

Once I reached the arbor I slowed my pace, remembering Miss Bingham's labored steps. I was appalled to think a woman of her age would indulge in such foolishness. At the school she had charge of young girls, some of whom might be easily enticed into following the destructive path of wickedness. Somehow there had to be a way to prevent that from happening. I didn't believe she was swayed by my aunt's money as much as she had been by Giles's good looks. My aunt knew how to get what she wanted, and she left no avenue unexplored.

I paused in the blackness. I could see nothing and reached out to my sides for guidance. My progress would be slow; however, I had only moved a few steps when Matthew whispered my name.

"Don't move," he said softly. "I will come to you."

"Are they all at the covenstead?"

"Yes." His speech became more clear as he approached. "The latch is still broken, and the door won't remain closed. Your aunt is quite upset about it, but it's good for us because it means we'll have a fairly clear view of the interior."

"Were you inside?"

"Yes. So was George Ambrus, though he didn't see me."

"I wonder why he came back."

"I don't know. He didn't linger, but walked around the outside in a contemplative manner. I wonder how long it's been there."

"As long as my aunt's been here, I would imagine. I learned from Francine that the aunt who raised Mama and her was also a witch. Francine also confided in me today that she wants to escape just as I do, but she's understandably afraid."

"My darling, before I say anything more, I want my arms around you."

As he spoke, he took my hands and placed them on his shoulders. His arms enclosed my waist as he drew me close. His heartbeat was as rapid as mine. My lips trembled beneath his, and a sob escaped my throat at the sheer ecstasy of our love. We clung to each other, and he whispered my name over and over as he rained kisses on my face.

He stepped back reluctantly and remained silent for a few moments. "There's a bench alongside us. I have a few things I wish to tell you before we watch the ceremony," he finally said, breaking the silence.

Once seated, I replied, "I know about Mrs. Ambrus. Miss Bingham said it was all anyone at the inn talked about."

"Yes," Matthew said resignedly. "A horrible death."

"My aunt was responsible. Pierce was sent to exert his powers. I have no idea whether he actually set the fire with his power. Perhaps he used a flammable substance. As for Miss Bingham, she is to be initiated tonight—married to Giles. My aunt purchased Miss Bingham's school, where she and Giles will live and get recruits to carry out their evil deeds."

"That's dreadful news," Matthew's tone expressed his revulsion.

"I also learned from Francine that my aunt was instrumental in causing my parents' death."

"I spent the night reading all I could find in the library about witchcraft."

"What did you learn?" I asked, fearful yet eager to know.

"Quite a lot. There are believers and disbelievers."

"Please don't say you don't believe me."

"No, my love. I've seen what they can do. I despise them, and I intend to get you out of here."

"I want to leave this place as quickly as possible, but not before I know you and your parents are safe. My aunt will stop at nothing to get revenge."

"The villagers are angered by what happened to Mrs. Ambrus. It seems your aunt has carried her vicious schemes too far."

"She warned me that something would happen to

you if I didn't marry Peter. They wanted Peter to initiate me tonight."

"Oh, my God," Matthew said angrily. "Are you sure they won't harm you?"

"No," I replied. "But don't forget, I too am a witch, and when my aunt revealed herself for what she is, I stood up to her. She didn't expect that. Nor did she expect my power to be greater than Giles's."

"Does she know you are aware of what she did to your parents?"

"No."

"It is better for her not to know. She might still believe you can be persuaded to join the coven. Please, if you love me, don't."

"Have no fear of that," I said. "I must outsmart her in some way, though I haven't figured out just how to do it. Did you know that she hates your parents?"

The blackness was so intense I could only imagine the surprise that etched his features. "She's quite an actress, isn't she?"

"I think "superb" would be the proper adjective to describe her talent. She expressed her regrets that she had brought me to the inn."

"Because of me," Matthew said. "I'm delighted she made that mistake. I love you, Nila. Say you will marry me."

"Please be patient," I pleaded. "I must do something to remove the evil from that mansion. It has to be stopped before it spreads. I am thinking of you and your parents and the students who will attend Miss Bingham's school. I'll not rest easy until everyone is safe. Oh, yes. Dulcy Lavery, Pierce's wife, said my aunt is going to punish George Ambrus. You must warn him."

"I will alert him and assure him you are no part of this. Now let us go and see them indulge in their satanic rites."

"I haven't heard my aunt mention satanism, but it must be related."

"The altar draped in black *is* part of it," Matthew said.

He guided me to the path. We traversed it carefully, pausing only when we reached the clearing. The door was open.

"There is no need to go closer," he said. "The light reflects their faces, and we can see the circle on the floor."

The smell of incense reached us, and I could see my aunt and Giles standing before the altar. She picked up the sword and handed it to him. He went over to where Miss Bingham stood, just outside the circle, still blindfolded. Her back was to us as he touched the tip of the sword to her chest and mouthed some words. She replied and nodded her head.

Francine moved into our line of vision and slipped her hands beneath Miss Bingham's robe, apparently freeing her bindings. Then Francine loosened the cloth blindfold while Miss Bingham slipped her hands into the sleeves of the robe and, still with her back to us, extended her upturned hands to accept the sword.

As she turned, the candles caught the gleam of the sword, sending shafts of light about the room. The others now surrounded the circle. Miss Bingham stepped inside the double circle, bent, placed the sword on the ground, then straightened and stood motionless. Giles bent to kiss her feet, then straightened and mouthed some words. When she replied, his hands loosed her robe, letting it fall to the ground.

"Come, Nila, you've seen enough to know the depravity to which they stoop. You're coming with me," Matthew commanded.

He turned me around and stepped ahead of me, placing his hands behind him for me to grasp so I could follow without straying off the path.

We didn't speak until we reached the end of the path. "You're not setting foot in that house again."

"I must go back." I was appalled by what I'd seen, but knew now my aunt would stop at nothing. She had to be mentally ill to be a party to such corruption. I'm terrified of what she will do to you and your parents."

"She will do nothing to us," Matthew replied firmly. "I will threaten to expose her."

"She will laugh at you. There are too many forces working against us."

"I'm not afraid of her, Nila. I will never let her harm you."

"She deliberately killed my parents. Mama once told me that at the time of Papa's death, he had had an offer from a famous university. It would have meant a tremendous increase in salary and prestige for him. He was financially poor, but rich in knowledge."

"I wish I could have met you before your aunt resorted to murder."

"So do I. It's ironic that she introduced us. Did you walk here?"

"At midday I walked through the forest to the estate. I spent some time studying the covenstead. I knew what each of the instruments on the altar was meant for, because I had sat up most of the night reading about witchcraft. Around five I returned to the inn for dinner and got a buggy to come back here."

"Where is it?"

"Hidden in the bushes just beyond the estate. You're coming back with me. I'll not allow you to return to the mansion."

I didn't argue, but had misgivings. "What will you tell your parents?"

"Nothing, at the moment. They left for Boston this morning and won't return for a few days."

"I have no change of clothing."

"You may use my parents' suite. And mother's your size, wouldn't you say?"

House of Silence

"Yes. Her figure is very youthful."

"Don't tell her I said so, but she's quite vain about it."

"She has a right to be." We both laughed. It was an outlet for our nervous tension.

We slowed down when we reached the road, since we had witnessed only the start of the ceremony and didn't need to hurry. Miss Bingham's features had been rapturous in anticipation. My aunt had smugly observed the initiation, knowing she had achieved another triumph. Up until now, Miss Bingham had been the epitome of respectability. She must never be allowed to return to the academy.

We were silent on the way back to the inn. The proceedings had been a shock to both of us. I thought of Francine and felt compassion for her. She wanted to disentangle herself from this web of iniquity, yet didn't know how. Matthew and I would have to help her.

It was a relief to enter the cheery inn. Matthew brought me to his parents' suite immediately. He told me to feel free to search the closets for some clothes.

He suggested I return to the lobby as soon as I had freshened up. He was going to order a few sandwiches and hot chocolate. It sounded delicious, and I promised I would join him shortly.

The small wardrobe I had brought to my aunt's would have to stay there. I would never return to that house of corruption. I did want the trunk with the mementos of Mama and Papa, but would wait awhile, fearful lest my aunt destroy its contents once she realized how much it meant to me.

After washing my hands and face, I went to the lobby and sought out the dining alcove. Matthew was already there with the food and beverage. After he seated me, I started to tell him what I had learned.

"Darling," he said kindly, "I want to know it all, but first you must eat. You may not realize it, but you're trembling."

We were seated side by side, and I raised my head and kissed his cheek. His arms enclosed me, and our lips met once again. However, I soon slipped free of his arms, for I was too concerned with the grave problem at hand.

"We can make love later, darling," I said softly. "I hunger for it as much as you. But, as you said, food is what I need now. While we're eating, I can tell you how wicked my aunt really is."

He gave a brief nod of his head. "Very well."

I related all my aunt had told me, then moved on to what I had learned from Francine. Matthew listened intently, nodding his head from time to time at the shocking story.

"You must find George Ambrus," I said, "and warn him. My aunt will not allow him to live after he embarrassed her at the inn. The fact that she had his mother burned to death doesn't lessen her hatred for George."

"He doesn't have a home," Matthew reflected. "Unless one of the villagers took pity on him."

"Couldn't he remain here and work for his board?"

"Yes," Matthew said. "I'll mention it to him. I think the most likely place to find him is at the mortician's. I'll go there tomorrow morning. Services for his mother will be held in the afternoon."

"Speaking of services, I wonder if the reason my aunt didn't come to Mama's funeral is that a witch does not set foot in a church."

"I read that witches fear the church, the cross, and any man who teaches the word of God."

"That also explains Miss Bingham's excusing herself at the last minute."

"Were you the only mourner?" Matthew asked.

"Yes. I don't know how Mama would have reacted had she known Miss Bingham had been following my aunt's orders since Papa died."

I told Matthew about Papa having received an opportunity for promotion just before his death.

House of Silence

"That probably frightened your aunt," Matthew reasoned. "She certainly could not have bribed a reputable university. Miss Bingham could be coerced more easily. Your aunt kept close tabs on you. When you were graduated, she felt the time had come to initiate you into the practice of witchcraft, and she could do so only by getting rid of your mother."

"I know now why Mama told me not to come up here. She was dying when she said that, but I believe she knew who killed Papa."

"What I want you to do now is to stop thinking of that place," Matthew said. "You must tell yourself that they cannot harm you."

"It's you and your parents I'm worried about. You saw what happened to your mother."

"Let's go on the premise that they know you will have nothing to do with black magic. Therefore, they are powerless to do anything to you or my family."

"I wish I could dismiss it as lightly as you," I said.

"You must," he replied seriously. "Only in that way can you shake off your fear. You are the strong one, Nila."

"Thank you, my love." His logic was inspiring. "I will do as you suggest."

"Promise?"

"I promise."

"Then your problems are ended. You are out of that house. The course is clear. The sooner we get married, the better. I've been a bachelor much too long."

"Are you absolutely certain?"

"Absolutely. And don't start on that subject again."

"I won't ever again. I'm going to convince myself that I am no different than anyone else."

"To me, you aren't. Now I will escort you to my parents' suite. We'll discuss our marriage tomorrow, after I talk with George at the mortician's. Now you need to rest. Would you like a sedative to help you sleep? I can summon Dr. Hebert."

"I don't need a thing." Then I slipped my arm around him. "I'll sleep like a babe, knowing you are close by. I feel as if a great weight has been lifted from me."

We kissed good night, and I stepped into his parents' suite, closing the door behind me. I leaned against it, reveling in the fact that I loved and was loved. My lips still felt the blissful touch of his, and I thrilled at the joy of what the future held for both of us. I knew Mama would be happy, knowing I was under Matthew's protection.

I found a nightgown and undressed, still filled with the ecstasy of Matthew's kiss. I slipped between the sheets and was asleep in minutes.

TEN

To my consternation, I didn't awaken until after ten o'clock. I dressed and went directly to the dining room, hoping to find Matthew. The clerk at the desk told me that he had left a message that he would return as quickly as possible. He added that breakfast would be served in the family dining room whenever I wished.

"When did Mr. Arneil leave?"

"Around eight o'clock this morning, Miss Parris," he replied. "He was going to the mortician's."

"Thank you." I went to the dining room, where a waitress was already serving my breakfast.

I had slept well and should have felt bright and cheerful, especially knowing that Matthew and I would soon be wed. Yet I was fighting a depression that grew with each minute, augmented by a gnawing fear for Matthew's safety. I was so relieved last night to escape my aunt's house that I had let him convince me our troubles had ended. In the cold light of day, I realized how wrong I was. Matthew and his parents were in as much danger as George Ambrus. My coming here had made them more vulnerable.

I wasn't even surprised when I heard a sound and looked up to see my aunt standing there. Faint scorn was evident as she regarded me.

"Good morning, Nila," she said graciously as she seated herself. "I've sent Giles to the mortician's to pay Mrs. Ambrus's funeral expenses."

Dorothy Daniels

The waitress returned and looked at her in surprise.

"Would you like some breakfast, Auntie?" I asked, determined not to make a scene, and hoping I could persuade her to be compassionate.

"Just coffee, please." She addressed the waitress. "I believe you're the young lady who served my niece and me the other day."

"Yes, ma'am," the waitress replied graciously. "I wanted to thank you for the very generous tip."

"You're quite welcome, my dear," my aunt replied. She radiated charm. I sensed my aunt was using the power she possessed to force me to return with her. I was determined to defy her, no matter what.

The waitress set a cup and saucer in front of my aunt and poured coffee for both of us. My aunt opened her handbag and pressed a bill into the waitress's hand.

"I can't, ma'am," the waitress replied, embarrassed by the gesture. "This is the family dining room."

"I know," my aunt said, smiling up at her. "But we are not family, and you deserve recompense. I am sure my niece will agree."

It was my turn to smile up at the waitress. "Whether I do or not, it doesn't pay to defy my aunt."

The waitress had no idea that I had hostile feelings toward my aunt. She took my statement as a suggestion that she should accept the gratuity.

After she left, my aunt regarded me from across the table. Her graciousness was gone now that there was no further need for it. I met her gaze as I sipped the hot coffee. My aunt never once took her eyes from my face, and I soon tired of the charade.

"Why did you come here?" I asked coldly.

"To bring you to your senses," she said.

"I am going to marry Matthew Arneil," I said firmly.

"A pity I wasn't aware of his intentions last night, or he would never have made the journey to my home safely."

House of Silence

"You destroy everyone who crosses you, don't you?"

"I usually don't need to," she said. "But I have yet to lose a battle."

"I am not fighting you, Auntie," I said. "I just don't want to have anything to do with you. I know now why Mama hated you."

Her smile was cynical. "I'm not surprised you do. I'm rather of the opinion that someone told you about your parents."

"I didn't need to be told. I saw you go to the covenstead last night. I followed and observed part of the ritual through the door that wouldn't close."

"That has been rectified."

"A pity that place didn't burn down instead of Mrs. Ambrus's home. As for sending Giles to the mortician's to pay for Mrs. Ambrus's funeral expenses, Matthew is there now attending to it. I doubt George Ambrus would allow you to pay. You must know the extent of his contempt for you."

"And for you," she said. "You can't be like the others, Nila. Come back with me."

"I will never go back to such depravity. Matthew and I are to wed very soon."

"No, my dear. You will wed Peter after your initiation. The ceremony, as you know, is essentially the marriage."

"I will never marry him. It will be Matthew or nobody."

"Then it will be nobody. I think that about now Matthew is not feeling very well. He has a fever of some sort, which will become more severe with chills and delirium. The doctor will be at a loss as to the cause, and you will be thought mad should you say Giles caused it."

"You wouldn't." My words were scarcely audible. I knew now the reason for the dejection which had consumed me this morning. The forces of evil had been at work from the moment my aunt found I was no longer in her home.

"I would. If you love Matthew enough to want him to live, come back. You belong there." Her smile was derisive. "I believe Loretta knew you were like me."

"No," I exclaimed angrily. "Mama was goodness. If she had lived, she would have told me about the curse."

"It's a gift, my dear." She picked up her cup and held it toward me. "More coffee, please. People fear us, and because they do, they dare not disobey."

I spoke as I poured. "Does Miss Bingham have the gift? Or are you just using her to get recruits?"

"She's radiant now that she is wed to Giles," my aunt said reflectively. "It will be good for her to go back to the school looking as she does."

I regarded her with disgust. "Is there no limit to your depravity? I will state here and now that I intend to inform the parents of every student that their daughters are in grave danger of being seduced into a life of corruption."

"I doubt they would believe you. You see, you are no longer there. Your mama did a stupid thing when she stepped in front of the van."

"Mama said it was stupid. I believe at the end she knew you were behind both it and Papa's drowning. I also believe you came to the hospital to hasten her end so she couldn't tell me about you."

"I did," my aunt said placidly. "I could not have her wrecking my plans. I need you. Despite what you think of me, you must come back. I *will* get you back, one way or another. You cannot escape. You must carry on the line. It's all I live for. Peter will be an excellent husband. He is fond of you and plans to take you as his wife tonight."

"I am not fond of him."

"Such handsomeness—and a splendid physique. He could stir you to the heights of ecstasy."

144

House of Silence

"That's enough, Auntie. You can sit here all day and argue, but I will never set foot in your house again."

She was about to say something, but instead pressed her fingers to her temples. Pain etched her features.

"May I get you something, Auntie?"

"No, my dear. Another of those headaches. I must go. You have no choice but to return. Don't delay too long, for Matthew's sake. I could also add, for mine."

"You are referring to your headaches," I said.

"Yes. I am almost never free of them now. But I will not die until you have taken my place as high priestess, with Peter as the high priest."

"What about Giles?"

"I want young blood. Besides, Giles will be busy at the school. He still has his looks and a charm that young ladies find irresistible."

"What about Miss Bingham?"

"Oh, she'll be his dutiful wife. She is quite impressed with being a member of the coven. Besides, she has been beholden to me for years."

"With the fees she charges, I should think she would be quite independent financially."

"Her brother was a good manager, but she was not. When he died, there was a large mortgage. I paid that off and saw to it there were sufficient sums at hand to run the school profitably. Of course, now I own it."

"Why didn't you let Mama know we weren't beholden to Miss Bingham?"

"Your mother was too clever."

"Mama told me that just before Papa died, he had gotten an offer from a university for a prestigious and important post."

"Miss Bingham wrote me about it. I had to act."

"So you admit you killed my parents."

"They had served their purpose. Once you were graduated, the time was ripe to instruct you in the rites which have been handed down in our family for generations."

I had scarcely touched my food. "Auntie, I have a headache now."

"Perhaps you will inherit those also."

"I hope not. I can see you are in great pain. You're pale."

"Not as pale as Matthew is at the moment. I believe he's taken a chill."

"Auntie, please." I reached out and grasped her wrist. "Don't hurt him."

"I am not even near him, my dear." She shook her arm free of my hand. "You'll come around. You'll be back—if you value Matthew's life."

"I'll do anything, Auntie, except be a part of witchcraft. It's evil. I can't submit."

"You have no choice. A pity the Arneils are away, or I would pay my respects to them. Do tell them I wish them well."

"You don't," I said solemnly. "You wish only your own kind well."

"For once you make sense. And since you are one of my kind, I wish you well."

She reached for her parasol and left the room. I toyed with my breakfast, but I was filled with the horror of what Matthew would be forced to suffer and had little appetite.

I returned to Mr. and Mrs. Arneil's suite. I didn't know what step to take next. I thought of going to the mortician's, but if Giles was there and saw me, he might turn on Matthew. I decided to ask the desk clerk where the mortician's was and go there immediately. I would exercise my powers once more for the sake of my beloved.

However, I had just reached the desk when a gentleman came running into the lobby, going directly to the desk clerk.

"Adam, you'd better get Dr. Hebert." he said. "Mr.

House of Silence

Arneil collapsed at the funeral home, and they're bringing him in."

Adam ran up the wide stairway, taking two steps at a time. I went to the screen doors, where I saw two men carrying the stretcher. Matthew was moaning softly, and his eyes were closed.

Two guests held the doors open. I told them to follow me to Matthew's suite. As we entered, the maid was just putting on the bedspread. I motioned her aside and drew down the bedclothes. It took four men to lift Matthew onto the bed.

At that moment, Dr. Hebert entered the room. He took Matthew's pulse and raised his eyelids.

"Is he unconscious, Doctor?"

"Yes," Dr. Hebert said. He placed a hand on Matthew's brow. "What happened?"

I knew, but before I spoke one of the men who had carried Matthew on the stretcher said, "He was at Jim Rogan's place and was talking to George Ambrus. Another man came in and spoke to Mr. Arneil. They seemed friendly enough, but without rhyme or reason, Mr. Arneil fainted. He'd seemed perfectly all right up until that minute."

"Do you work there?" I asked.

"Yes, miss. I help Mr. Rogan. I didn't know the other man who came in."

I described Giles.

"That's him, miss."

Dr. Hebert said, "Miss Parris, I must ask you to step into the corridor. I want to make a more thorough examination of Matthew."

"Yes, Doctor. May I come back and sit at his bedside?"

"You may." He spoke with quiet competence.

I went into the hall and sat on a bench just beyond the door. I would try everything in my power to bring Matthew out of the spell Giles had cast upon him. I dared not let my thoughts dwell on my aunt's threatening words.

I had no idea of how to cast a spell, but I wanted desperately to help Matthew. I would do everything possible—short of returning to that house. Yet what if his condition worsened? My aunt had said if I wished to spare him, I would have to return and marry Peter. Their horrible ceremonial rites repelled me. Yet if Matthew didn't improve, I would not have a choice. Nevertheless, I couldn't see myself going back there. Dr. Hebert would use every medical skill he possessed to cure Matthew. Surely he was more learned than any witch.

Dr. Hebert finally opened the door. The other gentlemen departed, and he beckoned me to come in. He said, "I've given Matthew a thorough examination. I'm completely puzzled. He has a fever and chills and is now delirious. I'm gravely concerned and feel his parents should be notified."

The news terrified me. "He was perfectly well last night. We were together until midnight."

"I breakfasted with him this morning," Dr. Hebert said. "He said nothing about not feeling well. His concern was for George Ambrus. Matthew wanted George to know he could room here and work at the new inn."

"I knew he was going to the mortician's to talk to George and take care of the funeral expenses."

Dr. Hebert nodded. "That isn't surprising. I'm going to let you sit by his bedside until I get a nurse. I suggest you keep cool cloths on his brow. He's very restless. Something inside seems to be driving him. He's calm at the moment, but those spells come and go. Matthew resisted my efforts to examine him. The men had to hold him down and may have to again. Call if he gets delirious and tries to fight you."

I gave my assurance, and Dr. Hebert headed for the door. "I'll have a nurse here shortly."

House of Silence

"Thank you, Doctor." I found a basin in the bathroom and filled it with cold water. I brought it into the bedroom, along with two washcloths, one of which I folded and placed across Matthew's brow. Just then his arms came up, and his hands thrust me away so hard that I fell backward against the wall.

He sat up and yelled obscenities. One man looked in the door and called for help. The men got Matthew down on the bed, but they had to hold him there until he exhausted himself.

Dr. Hebert came back into the room. "I was still outside. What happened?"

I explained as best I could, fighting to hold back the tears. I didn't tell the exact truth, stating that his words were garbled. Since neither of the two men that came running in disagreed with me, I gathered they hadn't heard.

"You can't remain in here, Miss Parris," Dr. Hebert said. "He might injure you. He has no awareness of where he is or what he is doing."

"I must stay here," I said. I was already begging Matthew to wake up, doing my best to fight the evil which had been cast over him. But I wasn't strong enough this time. Was it because I had renounced witchcraft? I couldn't pretend to embrace it. I had promised Matthew I would stop thinking about it.

Dr. Hebert placed an arm about my shoulder. "You're in a highly agitated state yourself. You won't help Matthew by remaining here. Doctors discourage loved ones from caring for their own. Matthew spoke of you briefly this morning. I know he loves you. You'll do him more good by leaving, especially now that the nurse has arrived."

A middle-aged lady in white had just entered. She went directly to Dr. Hebert.

He repeated, "Please, Miss Parris. Leave this to Miss Willett and me."

I nodded and left the room. There was nothing else

I could do without making a scene. I decided to fight evil with prayer.

Occasionally, Miss Willett came out to report that her patient's condition remained unchanged.

"Is he still delirious?" I asked.

"From time to time," she said. "What concerns Dr. Hebert most is Mr. Arneil's fever. It has risen higher since this morning. As for you, Miss Parris, you should get some lunch, or we'll have two patients on our hands."

"I'm not hungry, and I'm too upset to eat."

She said softly, "We're doing everything we can for him. Dr. Hebert will remain in the corridor all night."

"It isn't hopeless, is it?" I asked fearfully.

"There is always hope," she said encouragingly, though I sensed she made the statement only to lift my spirits.

She was gone a few minutes when the waitress arrived with a small tray. "I brought you some cucumber sandwiches and a glass of milk. Please drink it, Miss Parris. You look ill, and when the fever breaks, he'll need your smiling face."

"Thank you. What's your name?"

"Star Ingram. Too bad your aunt isn't here. She would be a help just now."

"I prefer being by myself. Thank you for these sandwiches."

"You're welcome, Miss Parris. Nurse Willett had a hand in it, too."

And so the day went. Dr. Hebert and Nurse Willett would come to Mr. and Mrs. Arneil's suite often and tell me there had been no change. The fever wouldn't break, and Matthew still had spells of delirium, which grew shorter as he became weaker.

When I heard that, I knew I had no choice but to return to the house. I was fully aware that Dr. Hebert hadn't the faintest idea of how to treat the illness. He

House of Silence

had sent a telegram to Matthew's parents in Boston, suggesting that they return immediately.

I didn't disturb either Nurse Willett or Dr. Hebert. Instead, I left word at the desk for Dr. Hebert that I had gone to my aunt's. Adam ordered a buggy for me, which I drove myself. I couldn't think of anything but Matthew. I didn't know how I could carry out such a venture, but if it came to Matthew's life or my honor, I knew the latter had to be sacrificed.

ELEVEN

Pierce opened the door when I pulled up before the entrance. I told him to return the horse and buggy to the inn. He looked pleased and informed me my aunt awaited me in her suite.

I went upstairs and confronted Francine, who nodded a greeting, at the same time placing her forefinger to her lips in a gesture of silence.

The window shades were lowered, but my aunt called to me from the bedroom.

I went to her, moving slowly around chairs and a table to the bed, where my aunt was propped up on several pillows.

"Welcome home, Nila," she said.

I dispensed with formality and got to the point. "Matthew is gravely ill. I came to beg you to be merciful and cast off the evil spell."

"That was Giles's doing," she replied softly. Obviously, it was even painful for her to talk. I had to strain my ears to hear her.

"You ordered him to do it."

"True. I told you he would be taken ill. Unless you do as I ask, Matthew will die at dawn tomorrow."

"You wouldn't."

"I would," came the whispered reply.

"Why?"

"We've been over that," she said. "If you want him to live, you will be initiated into our coven tonight. After the ceremony, you will be Peter's wife."

House of Silence

"No court of law would recognize such a marriage," I said disdainfully.

"We have our own laws and expect strict obedience. You must make up your mind at once."

"The very thought of such self-debasement repels me."

"It is up to you. Matthew's life will depend on your decision."

'You make the decisions in this house." I couldn't keep despair from my voice. "Death means little to you when it is someone else's."

"My own will come, once you have been made high priestess," she said. "I believe I have a dreadful sickness in my head."

"Perhaps the sickness is what makes you perform such evil deeds."

"You tire me, child. Go. I will rest until this evening. We will await you at the coven at nine. If you do not come, we will call down the curse upon Matthew and demand his life."

I couldn't answer. As much as I loved Matthew, I could not defile my body in such fashion. There had to be another way.

I turned and left the room, taking care to open and close the door of the suite noiselessly. Despite my revulsion for this woman, I was sorry she suffered such torture from her headaches.

I went to my suite and sat down. A soft tap sounded on the door, and I reached out and turned the knob.

Francine stepped in and closed the door behind her. "Mademoiselle, I cannot stay long. I was sent here, but I want to say that I am sorry for your heartbreak."

"Thank you, Francine." I couldn't even manage a smile. I was numb. I was devoid of feeling, knowing my mission had met with failure. My aunt was relentless, determined to carry on the line of witches. I must marry Peter—if it could be called marriage. Mama had raised me with a high regard for morality, and I could not turn my back on that now. Yet the mere thought of Matthew dying was more than I could bear.

"You know he will die, mademoiselle, if you do not obey," Francine said.

"My aunt made that quite clear this morning."

"You must be initiated tonight by Peter."

"I cannot."

"You are brave. It takes much courage to refuse."

"No, Francine. I'm a coward. If I were brave, I would go through with the ceremony—even if I hate Peter. Afterward, I would go mad with shame."

"Yes. I believe you would. You know your aunt is very sick in her head." Francine touched her brow.

"I think the pain has crazed her."

"It could be," Francine agreed. "But she is wicked anyway. She allows no one to stand in her way. Not you. Not your beloved."

"And not my parents," I said, for the first time showing a trace of spirit.

"I came to ask if you would like something to eat."

"Nothing, thanks. Is dinner being served downstairs?"

"No. Everyone is eating in their rooms tonight. Your aunt believes you will come to the covenstead. She sent me in to lay out your robe."

"You must obey her, Francine. Even Dulcy was afraid not to."

"Everyone is afraid of your aunt."

"What about Giles?"

"He, too. His foolish wife is strutting around the house like a peacock."

"She isn't really his wife."

"In witchcraft she is."

"She is foolish."

"But dedicated. She already knows every rule from the *Book of Shadows*."

"Perhaps I should look at them. I might learn something, too."

"How do you mean that, mademoiselle?" Francine asked, eyeing me curiously.

"It would be wiser for me not to tell you," I said. "Then you wouldn't get in trouble."

"I am in trouble," she replied with a trace of embarrassment. "I pleaded with your aunt for your happiness. She got angry. I brought on her headache."

"If she is so ill, how can she go to the covenstead?"

"She takes medication for her pain."

"When was my absence discovered?"

"Early this morning. I was sent here by your aunt to summon you."

"For what reason?"

"She wanted to tell you what was to happen to Matthew because you didn't attend the ceremonial rites last night."

"It would have happened even if I hadn't gone with him last night?"

She gave a slow nod of her head.

"There must be something I can do," I exclaimed. "I can't let him die."

"Mademoiselle, if I say something," she spoke hesitantly, "promise you will not get angry."

"Of course I won't."

"You forget something very important. You too are a witch. You too can call down a curse."

"I don't understand."

She cast a hasty glance at the door, opened it, and looked down the length of the corridor. "I cannot stay. I think Dulcy and Pierce are spying on me."

"What about Peter?"

"I doubt it. He is playing tennis with Giles. The bride is watching."

We both gave a knowing nod. "Go on, Francine."

"Go tonight. Call down a curse on them."

"What kind of curse?"

155

She shrugged and lowered her voice to a whisper. "You can threaten them."

"I couldn't," I exclaimed. "That would be horrible."

"No more so than what they have done."

"But I'm not like them."

"You had better try to be, at least for a little while. Think about it, mademoiselle. And one thing more. Your aunt said no clothes under the robe. Also no shoes or stockings. What do I tell her? I have to return with an answer."

"I don't know if I can, Francine."

"Your aunt says you have no choice. I agree, but for a different reason. It is up to you now. You have a life in your hands."

"That isn't true. My aunt has."

"Yes," Francine agreed. "They believe they are seven against one. They are six. Whatever curse you call down, I will take your side."

"They will destroy you," I exclaimed.

"I destroyed myself long ago," she replied. "I cannot go back to my beloved Paris. I am ashamed for all the bad things I've done. Only you can end it. Think hard, mademoiselle. Your aunt destroyed your mother and father. Do not let her destroy you and the man you love."

"I will think about it, Francine," I said.

"You have one hour. It is eight o'clock. At nine your initiation starts. Now it is up to you. I can remain no longer. Good luck."

She disappeared into the bedroom to place the robe on the bed and then left.

I sat there as dusk settled into night. I wouldn't go down to the covenstead on the lower floor. I had no desire to read the rules in the *Book of Shadows*. I hadn't needed the book to save the life of the puppy or to bring Mrs. Arneil out of Giles's evil spell.

None of them but Francine knew the true meaning

House of Silence

of love. They cared for nothing except their rites, which they practiced under the pretense of witchcraft.

I got up reluctantly and lit a small lamp. I was sick inside at what I had to do, yet I knew Matthew was fading. He was helpless in the spell they had cast on him. I had to go to the covenstead. I wouldn't let them go unchallenged. Nor would I let Matthew die.

I went into the bedroom and undressed. I had to stop thinking or I might weaken and not go. I picked up the robe and slipped my arms into it, making certain the braided belt was fastened securely.

I wanted to pray for success, but my mission was so corrupt I dared not. I must succeed or fail on my own initiative.

I went to the bedroom window, which gave a clear view of the estate. Miss Bingham and Giles came into view, wearing the ceremonial garment. Her arm was around his waist, and as I watched, she swung around to face him, placed her arms around his neck, and drew his head down to hers. I turned away from their wanton kiss. I could not let those two return to the school and carry out their wicked plans. My aunt had completely corrupted Miss Bingham, and I understood better what Francine had said a short time ago. One day, when Miss Bingham came to her senses, she would be as filled with self-loathing as Francine was.

I imagined that the others were already there, so I decided to get started. The full moon was in evidence as I left the house. I knew that the rites were carried out at this time of month.

I entered the arbor and slowed, for it was impossible to see far, and I didn't want to scrape my shins on one of the benches. There was no Matthew to guide me to the path, though I felt I knew where it was.

I found it without the slightest trouble, and was just about to follow it when a hand clamped over my mouth and an arm went around my waist. I was pulled back into the arbor and struggled helplessly. Whoever held me was strong. I knew it was a man, though just who it might be I had no idea.

"Don't fight me. I mean you no harm. I came at the request of the man who told me this morning he loved you. I'm George Ambrus. Mr. Arneil told me you're not in with these others."

I suddenly ceased my struggles.

"Will you be quiet if I let you go, miss?"

I nodded, and he freed me. I couldn't see him, nor he me, but he must have had a good look at me as I moved down the lawn to the formal garden.

"Why did you come?" I asked.

"To save you. I went to the inn to see how Mr. Arneil was. I learned he was worse. I was told you had returned to your aunt's. An evil woman, she is."

"Yes. And she can do you great harm."

"I know that. But I'll take care to stay out of her sight. You're not goin' in there, are you?"

"I must. Matthew will die if I don't."

"You will die if you go in there. He told me what your aunt did to your parents, and we know what she did to my mother."

"That was horrible. I'm sorry about it."

"I don't think Mr. Arneil would like you to go in there."

"It's the only way I can save his life."

"Will you scream if you need help?"

"I will." I'd do no such thing, as he'd be no match for them.

"I'll lead you along the path. Take hold of my coat."

"Thank you, Mr. Ambrus."

We made our way carefully until we reached the clearing. I tapped him on the shoulder and whispered for him to remain behind.

"Good luck," he whispered.

I nodded my thanks and told him to leave this evil place.

House of Silence

"I'll wait a bit, Miss Nila. Go now. Try to save Matthew."

There was no time for argument. George Ambrus's statement about Matthew's condition was far from reassuring. I walked across the open area and depressed the latch on the door, but it didn't open. I then knocked several times.

Dulcy's voice asked for identification, which I gave, though I felt it was needless. Who else would come here?

I heard a board scrape against wood. Apparently they had a bar across the door. Did they suspect that George Ambrus was prowling the area? I hoped not, for his sake.

My aunt was at the altar. This time Giles and Miss Bingham formed the circle, along with Dulcy, Pierce, and Francine. All wore the robes, although the hoods had been slipped back. Peter stood beside my aunt at the altar, and his face lit up at the sight of me. The fact that I was wearing the garment was proof I would be willing to participate in the initiation rites.

My aunt smiled briefly as Peter came forward and extended his hand to me. I went along with the charade, though I dared not look at Francine, fearful my aunt might read something into it.

He led me to the altar. My aunt turned to Peter and placed the sword in his outstretched hands. He held it aloft and asked for my complete obedience. When I answered, he pressed the length of the sword against my chest and called on the powers to let the strength of my body pass into the sword. Then he handed me the sword, just as Matthew and I had watched Giles hand it to Miss Bingham last night.

Giles left the circle and went to the altar, where he touched a candle flame to a stick of incense. Then he took the short sword and returned to his place in the circle.

He raised his arm and held the sword toward the

roof of the covenstead. "Raise your sword as I have raised mine, Nila. Call upon the powers to let the strength flow into the sword, then through your body."

I obeyed, careful to hold the sword steady. The ceremony was no longer foolish or amusing, and I was frightened.

"Before Peter kneels before you," Giles went on, "you may speak to us as an equal. Tell us of the part you wish to play in our coven."

I looked over at Giles, who commanded me to keep my eyes on the sword. The heavy smell of incense was making me ill.

Miss Bingham smiled encouragement. "Do it, child. Obey my husband. He is high priest."

"Why should I, when Peter is going to replace him in that position of honor?" I asked.

She and Giles both regarded me with astonishment.

I managed a smile of disdain. "Ask my aunt, if you don't believe me."

"Is that true, Evelyn?" Giles asked, stunned by what I'd just said.

"Yes," my aunt replied. "You will live at the school. You know why."

"He could still be high priest," Miss Bingham said. "We could return here from time to time."

"You will start a coven of your own." My aunt regarded them coldly. "When the school reopens, you must waste no time in getting recruits. The girls will find it exciting."

Francine said, "They will also find Giles exciting."

"Be quiet, handmaiden." My aunt spoke sternly. "Make no trouble here. You had Giles. I could banish you from the coven. We will have no more talk that could set one witch or warlock against another. We are now going to dispose of Matthew."

"Why?" I cried out. "You told me that if I came, you would let him live."

House of Silence

"You told him too much," my aunt replied sternly. "He cannot live."

"I told him everything about you. But he will live."

"He is dying even now," she retorted scornfully.

"No. I call on my powers as a witch. I have drawn enough strength from the sword to make yours fruitless."

My aunt said, "There are seven of us and one of you."

Francine stepped into the circle. "Six of you. I will use my powers to thwart you."

"Grip the sword with me, Francine," I said. "Together we call on the powers to destroy everyone except the two of us the moment Matthew ceases to breathe."

"You cannot," my aunt exclaimed loudly. "I am the high priestess. My powers are stronger than anyone's."

"Even those of the high priest?" Giles asked.

"Yes," my aunt replied. "Don't be a fool, Giles. You are nothing without me."

"Once I would have agreed," he said. "I have done your bidding too many years. I will still do it at the academy, but I will not give up my position as high priest."

"You will," my aunt said firmly. "Peter will lead now as the husband of my niece. I insist. The line must be carried on. Because I was childless, Nila has been in my plans since her birth. You served your purpose, Giles. If you wish a roof over your head—and I am referring to the school—you and Clare Bingham had better obey."

"I am Mrs. Lazarno," Miss Bingham retorted indignantly. "Giles claimed me as his wife last night."

My aunt laughed disdainfully. "Only because I insisted. Look in your mirror, woman. Then look at Giles. How do you expect to hold him? Even now, he is amused by your foolishness. It was Francine before you, and many before her."

To my astonishment, Miss Bingham's eyes glistened with tears.

She switched her gaze to Francine. "Is that true, Francine?"

Francine lowered her eyes. One couldn't help but feel sympathy for Miss Bingham.

She repeated her question. "Is it, Francine?"

"Yes." Francine's reply was barely audible.

Miss Bingham dropped to her knees and covered her face with her hands. I wished Giles would raise her to her feet and place an arm about her. Instead, he eyed her with disgust.

Peter said, "For God's sake, are we going to have a ceremony or aren't we?"

"We are," my aunt replied. "As soon as we have called down the curse of death upon Matthew Arneil."

"The moment you do that," I said, "your fate will be sealed. The fate of every one of you in this room, with the exception of Francine and me, is to die. We have already called on our powers to destroy you."

Peter said, "Are you mad, Nila? Why should you care about what happens to Matthew Arnell?"

"I love him," I said.

Peter disputed that with, "Your aunt said it was merely an infatuation; that it was I with whom you wished to spend your life."

"How could you have believed her?" I asked. "Surely you must know she is ruthless."

Giles said, "She is also rich, and Peter likes money."

"Who gave you the courage to defy me?" my aunt asked angrily.

"Your niece has courage. I told her to defy you." Francine let go of the sword and faced my aunt.

"Come to the altar," my aunt commanded.

"Don't go, Francine," I pleaded. "The woman is mad."

"If I am," my aunt said, "it's because I'm crazed with pain."

House of Silence

Francine left the circle and walked up to my aunt. Before anyone dared to stop her, my aunt picked up a knife from the altar and plunged it into Francine's chest. For a moment Francine stood motionless, then her body slowly crumpled to the ground. I ran to her and cradled her in my arms. The blood was already soaking through her robe.

She managed to look up at me, though her eyes were already glazing. "I want to die. I could not live with my sins . . ." Her head fell to one side. She was dead.

I stared at my aunt, who was looking down at Francine triumphantly. "She defied me. No one does that and lives. Not even you, Nila."

She uttered a cry like that of a wounded animal and pressed her hands to her head. She fell to her knees, trying to grip the altar. Her hands grasped the cloth, but pulled it to the floor with her. The lighted candelabra fell, along with a large dish of oil, which immediately ignited. My aunt's robe went up in flames. She must have been unconscious—or dead—for she didn't even scream. I couldn't go near her, for the oil had engulfed not only the altar but the rug, and was already burning within the circle. I looked around and saw Dulcy and Pierce beating at the flames, trying to reach my aunt. Peter and Giles stood motionless and glassy-eyed. Miss Bingham still knelt with her hands covering her face. I wondered if my aunt had cast a spell on them.

"Get out," I screamed. "We'll all burn to death."

I ran for the door, opened it, and headed straight for the path. I believed the others would follow, but when I reached the end of the clearing, I looked over my shoulder and couldn't believe my eyes. The entire place was in flames. In front of the door were burning branches that must have been dropped from the roof.

I looked up and saw George torching branches and throwing them down. They seemed to explode. I didn't wonder when the odor of kerosene assailed my nostrils.

"George. George Ambrus," I cried out. "What have you done?"

"Go home, Miss Nila. Go home. You don't belong with the others. I have to burn them. I'll burn them the way they burned my mother."

"You'll burn, too," I cried. "Get down off there."

"What I'm doing is murder, miss. I have no desire to live. At least I know what I'm doin' is wrong. But I'm stoppin' them from committing further wrongs."

"Jump down. You won't get hurt. The fire hasn't spread yet."

"It will. I poured kerosene all around the place. Even on the roof. Go. Get away from this evil place. Only burning will cleanse it of all its evil. I'm happy, miss. I'm doin' good."

I didn't know it, but I was sobbing hysterically. I knew it was useless to plead with George. I saw the door open, sucking the flames inward. I heard cries of agony, then a shriek. I looked up on the roof. George Ambrus was a living torch. His screams were the loudest, but were short-lived. No one could exist in there. Why didn't they follow me? They could have gotten out when I did. I only knew I was the only witch that had escaped alive.

I stumbled along the path as tears impeded my vision. Once I reached the arbor, I used the sleeve of my robe to wipe my eyes. I had to get control of myself. I could smell the acrid smoke. I walked out of the arbor and saw the red sky.

I went home and up to my suite to change my clothes quickly. I left through the kitchen, went out the back door, and headed for the barn. Halfway there, I heard the sound of wagon wheels on the gravel drive. I turned back to the house, hoping it was someone who would give me a ride back to the inn.

I had just rounded the corner when the carriage pulled up.

"Nila. Nila, my darling." I couldn't believe my ears. Not until I could see him would I belive it was Matthew. He lost no time getting down, and the next moment we were in each other's arms, kissing, declaring our love for each other, and asking questions.

"Please, Matthew," I exclaimed, raising my voice. "How did you get well so fast?"

"It's as much a mystery to me as it is to Dr. Hebert," he said. "But a few minutes after I came out of that spell and learned where you were, I headed for the barn and got here as fast as I could."

"Don't you feel weak?" I asked.

He laughed heartily, placed his arms around my waist, and lifted me above his head. "Does this feel as if I am?"

"No," I exclaimed, smiling down at him. Sobering, I added, "I thought you were going to die."

"Everyone did, including Dr. Hebert. I understand he sent a telegram to my parents. I'm glad. They'll be present for our wedding, which will take place as soon as you consent. Tomorrow, if possible."

"Perhaps the day after," I said, recalling the grim events that had taken place minutes ago. "I have a revolting story to tell you. The covenstead burned down. George Ambrus didn't start the fire. My aunt collapsed, pulled down the cloth and oil from the altar, and the candles ignited the oil."

"What did George do?"

"He burned the place from the outside. I think he may have saved my life by doing so. I don't know. My aunt paid me a visit at the inn this morning while you were at the mortician's."

"While I was there, Giles stopped by to arrange to pay for the funeral expenses. I refused to let him. Right after that I became ill. But before he arrived, I'd talked to George."

"He told me. I spoke with him before I went to the covenstead. My aunt said you would die if I didn't join them. Francine reminded me that I was a witch and had the same powers as they. She said she would be on my side. She kept her word—and was murdered by my aunt. I think my aunt had some kind of malignant growth in her head. She had dreadful headaches, and a spell came over her right after she plunged a knife into Francine's chest."

"Why didn't the others escape?"

"I don't know. I told them to get out of there. When I ran out, I thought they were following. I don't think Giles would have allowed me to live. He was angry at the witches."

"Why?"

"My aunt was going to demote him. He could no longer be high priest, as Peter was to have that honor. I would have been high priestess of the coven. My aunt knew she was going to die. The headaches were with her almost constantly, and she had become addicted to the medicine."

Matthew drew me close. "It must have been a dreadful ordeal for you."

"It was. And I'm still a witch. I know it now because I put a curse on them. I told them the moment you died, they too would die. Francine stepped into the circle with me and called down the curse also. That was when my aunt attacked her."

"But you did put a curse on your aunt."

"Yes, I am a witch."

"You *were* a witch," Matthew said quietly. "I told you that I read up on witchcraft."

"Yes."

"I learned that when a witch puts a curse on another witch, she loses her powers. You have lost yours, my darling. You are as normal as the rest of us."

"Is that true?" I asked.

"Absolutely," he replied. "I have the book to show you."

House of Silence

"I don't want to look at it," I said. "The knowledge that I am free to marry you fills my heart with joy."

"And you will marry me?"

"Yes, my beloved Matthew."

"Now let me take you back to the inn. We have plans to make, but first you must rest. I don't want you to come back here."

"The only thing I want in this house is a trunk in the attic."

"All you'll need to do is tell me what is in it, and I'll see that it's brought to our home in Boston. We'll build a summer house here—unless you would rather not come back."

"I'm not afraid anymore. As for this place, why not turn it into a museum? Some of the paintings and statuary have been stolen and must be returned. The gardens and forests are wonderful for picnics."

Matthew had already lifted me into the carriage. I slipped my arm around his, rested my head on his shoulder, and didn't stir until we were at the inn. Neither of us spoke a word all the way back. We didn't need to. We were too filled with the wonder of our love.

Matthew attended to the funerals. There was little left to bury, for the place had been a pyre of death. George Ambrus's charred remains were buried beside his mother's.

Peter's remains were sent to his parents' home in Boston. The others, being pagans, had no church services, but Francine, who had renounced witchcraft when she joined me in calling down a curse on the others, was given a church burial. She had a tree-shaded spot in the cemetery next to the church. I only wish her life could have been spared. She was so young and good. However, I believe she had no further desire to live when she walked willingly toward my aunt, knowing as she did so that she would die.

The Arneils' attorney saw to it that the valuable paintings that had been stolen from various museums were returned. He did the same with statuary and other pieces of art and artifacts. But much of what was in the house was priceless, and had bills of sale to prove it had been purchased honestly.

The mansion is now a museum, with picnic grounds which are crowded during the summer season. Since my aunt had been so wealthy, I asked Matthew to see to it that all the mortgages that had been held by her be forgiven. I can walk the streets of the village and be greeted as one of the locals. And I do, enjoying every moment, and only wishing Mama were alive to enjoy this life with me.

Miss Bingham's Academy has been sold to a reputable group of educators who will continue its high standards.

Matthew and I are very happy, and his parents love me as much as they do their son. The story of my aunt had to come out, and for a while reporters came from all over the country to write about it.

Matthew and I gave interviews only once. No mention was made of the fact that I was once a witch. Nor did a single one of the villagers speak of it. They have always been wary of strangers, and the reporters were no exception.

It is all in the past now. Matthew and I purchased a home in Boston where we live in the winter. He is building a house next to the new inn, where we will spend our summers with our family, which has already been started. I expect a baby in a few months.

We never talk of the past. The only evidence left are Papa's paintings and various other mementos. The picture of my parents sits on a table in our parlor, as a reminder of only the good times in my life.

SIGNET Gothics by Caroline Farr

- [ ] **SECRET AT RAVENSWOOD** (#E9181—$1.75)*
- [ ] **ROOM OF SECRETS** (#E8965—$1.75)*
- [ ] **DARK CITADEL** (#Y7552—$1.25)
- [ ] **ISLAND OF EVIL** (#W8476—$1.50)*
- [ ] **SINISTER HOUSE** (#W7892—$1.50)
- [ ] **SIGNET DOUBLE GOTHIC—WITCHES' HAMMER and GRANITE FOLLY** (#J8360—$1.95)*
- [ ] **SIGNET DOUBLE GOTHIC—HOUSE OF DARK ILLUSION and THE SECRET OF THE CHATEAU** (#E7662—$1.75)
- [ ] **CASTLE ON THE LOCH** (#E8830—$1.75)*
- [ ] **CASTLE OF TERROR** (#E8900—$1.75)*

*Price slightly higher in Canada

Buy them at your local bookstore or use coupon on next page for ordering.

Big Bestsellers from SIGNET

- [ ] **ECSTASY'S EMPIRE** by Gimone Hall. (#E9292—$2.75)
- [ ] **FURY'S SUN, PASSION'S MOON** by Gimone Hall. (#E8748—$2.50)*
- [ ] **RAPTURE'S MISTRESS** by Gimone Hall. (#E8422—$2.25)*
- [ ] **HARVEST OF DESTINY** by Erica Lindley. (#J8919—$1.95)*
- [ ] **BELLADONNA** by Erica Lindley. (#J8387—$1.95)
- [ ] **DEVIL IN CRYSTAL** by Erica Lindley. (#E7643—$1.75)
- [ ] **GLYNDA** by Susannah Leigh. (#E8548—$2.50)*
- [ ] **WINTER FIRE** by Susannah Leigh. (#E8680—$2.50)
- [ ] **CALL THE DARKNESS LIGHT** by Nancy Zaroulis. (#E9291—$2.95)
- [ ] **THE RAGING WINDS OF HEAVEN** by June Lund Shiplett. (#E9439—$2.50)
- [ ] **REAP THE BITTER WINDS** by June Lund Shiplett. (#E9517—$2.50)
- [ ] **THE WILD STORMS OF HEAVEN** by June Lund Shiplett. (#E9063—$2.50)*
- [ ] **DEFY THE SAVAGE WINDS** by June Lund Shiplett. (#E9337—$2.50)*
- [ ] **CLAUDINE'S DAUGHTER** by Rosalind Laker. (#E9159—$2.25)*
- [ ] **WARWYCK'S WOMAN** by Rosalind Laker. (#E8813—$2.25)*
- [ ] **THE MONEYMAN** by Judith Liederman. (#E9164—$2.75)*

*Price slightly higher in Canada

Buy them at your local bookstore or use this convenient coupon for ordering.

THE NEW AMERICAN LIBRARY, INC.,
P.O. Box 999, Bergenfield, New Jersey 07621

Please send me the SIGNET BOOKS I have checked above. I am enclosing $_____ (please add 50¢ to this order to cover postage and handling). Send check or money order—no cash or C.O.D.'s. Prices and numbers are subject to change without notice.

Name _____

Address _____

City_____ State_____ Zip Code_____

Allow 4-6 weeks for delivery.
This offer is subject to withdrawal without notice.

More Bestsellers from SIGNET

- [ ] **THE HOUR BEFORE MIDNIGHT** by Velda Johnston.
  (#E9343—$2.25)
- [ ] **THE ETRUSCAN SMILE** by Velda Johnston. (#E9020—$2.25)
- [ ] **I CAME TO THE HIGHLANDS** by Velda Johnston.
  (#J8218—$1.95)
- [ ] **THE WHITE PAVILION** by Velda Johnston. (#J8700—$1.95)*
- [ ] **THE FRENCH BRIDE** by Evelyn Anthony. (#J7683—$1.95)
- [ ] **THE PERSIAN PRICE** by Evelyn Anthony. (#J7254—$1.95)†
- [ ] **THE POELLENBERG INHERITANCE** by Evelyn Anthony.
  (#E7838—$1.75)†
- [ ] **THE RETURN** by Evelyn Anthony. (#E8843—$2.50)†
- [ ] **THE SILVER FALCON** by Evelyn Anthony. (#E8211—$2.25)†
- [ ] **STRANGER AT THE GATE** by Evelyn Anthony.
  (#W6019—$1.50)†
- [ ] **VALENTINA** by Evelyn Anthony. (#E8598—$2.25)†
- [ ] **MISTRESS OF DESIRE** by Rochelle Larkin. (#E7964—$2.25)
- [ ] **TORCHES OF DESIRE** by Rochelle Larkin. (#E8511—$2.25)*
- [ ] **HARVEST OF DESIRE** by Rochelle Larkin. (#E8771—$2.25)
- [ ] **THIS IS THE HOUSE** by Deborah Hill. (#E8877—$2.50)
- [ ] **THE HOUSE OF KINGSLEY MERRICK** by Deborah Hill.
  (#E8918—$2.50)*

* Price slightly higher in Canada
† Not available in Canada

Buy them at your local
bookstore or use coupon
on next page for ordering.

SIGNET Books You'll Enjoy

- [ ] **THE PASSIONATE SAVAGE** by Constance Gluyas.
  (#E9195—$2.50)*
- [ ] **MADAM TUDOR** by Constance Gluyas. (#J8953—$1.95)*
- [ ] **THE HOUSE ON TWYFORD STREET** by Constance Gluyas.
  (#E8924—$2.25)*
- [ ] **FLAME OF THE SOUTH** by Constance Gluyas.
  (#E8648—$2.50)*
- [ ] **WOMAN OF FURY** by Constance Gluyas. (#E8075—$2.25)*
- [ ] **ROGUE'S MISTRESS** by Constance Gluyas. (#E8339—$2.25)
- [ ] **SAVAGE EDEN** by Constance Gluyas. (#E9285—$2.50)
- [ ] **OAKHURST** by Walter Reed Johnson. (#J7874—$1.95)
- [ ] **MISTRESS OF OAKHURST** by Walter Reed Johnson.
  (#J8253—$1.95)
- [ ] **LION OF OAKHURST** by Walter Reed Johnson.
  (#E8844—$2.25)*
- [ ] **FIRES OF OAKHURST** by Walter Reed Johnson.
  (#E9406—$2.50)
- [ ] **HOTEL TRANSYLVANIA** by Chelsea Quinn Yarbro.
  (#J8461—$1.95)*
- [ ] **THE PALACE** by Chelsea Quinn Yarbro. (#E8949—$2.25)*
- [ ] **SINS OF OMISSION** by Chelsea Quinn Yarbro.
  (#E9165—$2.25)*
- [ ] **BLOOD GAMES** by Chelsea Quinn Yarbro. (#E9405—$2.75)*

*Price slightly higher in Canada

Buy them at your local bookstore or use this convenient coupon for ordering.

THE NEW AMERICAN LIBRARY, INC.,
P.O. Box 999, Bergenfield, New Jersey 07621

Please send me the SIGNET BOOKS I have checked above. I am enclosing
$_____ (please add 50¢ to this order to cover postage and handling).
Send check or money order—no cash or C.O.D.'s. Prices and numbers are subject to change without notice.

Name _____

Address _____

City_____ State_____ Zip Code_____
Allow 4-6 weeks for delivery.
This offer is subject to withdrawal without notice.